HUNTER SECURITY BOOK FOUR

LAURA JOHN

Cover Designer: Brittany Franks with Chaotic Creatives

Editor: Swish Design and Editing

Sensitivity Reader: J.P Jacksonand Crystal Grizzard Burnette with Crystal Clear Author Services

To those who fall in love quickly.
Never change who you are.
Continue to love with all your heart!

Dear Reader,

This book touches on a few sensitive and heavy subjects that could be difficult for some to read.
If you think there is a subject that could be a problem for you, please proceed to my website for a complete list of content warnings.

Chapter One

ARCHER

Sᴡᴇᴀᴛ ɪs ᴘᴏᴜʀɪɴɢ ᴅᴏᴡɴ my back as I strut across the stage, singing to the thousands of people in the stadium. Bright lights are shining on me, and the roar of the crowd is so loud it almost drowns out my band, which has a smile permanently planted on my face.

This is what I live for.

"You've been amazing," I shout to the crowd, walking offstage to where my twin sister and manager, Aria, is waiting.

"You did so good," she cheers and pulls me into her arms.

"I always do," I brag with a wink.

Aria rolls her eyes and gives me a playful shove. "Good to see your ego is still intact. Wouldn't want that to fade."

"When you're this good, nothing can knock you down."

"Did you mistake the memo that said confidence is sexy for cockiness is sexy instead?" Brando, my drummer, asks.

I throw my head back and laugh. "What's the difference between the two?"

"Noncocky people know the difference," he says with a shit-eating grin before walking away.

"Jackass," I murmur under my breath.

Landon, my bass player, walks over to give me a high five. "We fucking killed it out there tonight," he states.

"We always do, but you're right. There was something special about tonight."

"It's because everything's better in Texas," Joseph, my guitar player, adds.

I give his shoulder a shove. "The saying is 'everything's bigger in Texas,' smartass. But I don't even know if that saying is true or not. I mean, you're from Texas, and you ain't that big," I tease.

"I might be short, but I'm not small," he retorts. "Want me to show you?" He moves to unbutton his jeans.

"Keep it in your pants. My sister doesn't need to see your little pecker," I chastise him, making him laugh.

"Sometimes I regret being your band manager," Aria murmurs.

"Because we're too awesome?" Joseph asks her.

"Yes... that's exactly the reason I was thinking," she responds dryly.

He chuckles and gives her a wet kiss on her cheek, then walks away.

I love my band so much. They are more than coworkers and friends. They're family.

"Okay, guys," Aria shouts. "Get changed quick. Once you're done, we'll make our way to the hotel. We're taking the private jet home tomorrow morning bright and early, so if you're going out after, don't get stupid drunk."

The guys and I acknowledge we heard my sister, then make our way to the dressing rooms. We are all eager to get to the hotel and waste no time getting ready, heading out within minutes of each other.

"I love touring, but I'm glad to have a bit of time off," I say as we are escorted out of the stadium to where our limo is waiting.

"It's probably because you're getting old," Brando tells me.

"Says the man who is five years older than me," I reply.

He shakes his head with a smile on his lips as he places his hands on his chest. "Yeah, but I'm young at heart."

As we reach the exit, the security team we hired for the night opens the door for us, and we're immediately greeted by a few fans and paparazzi. Waving at our fans, we smile and sign a few autographs.

"I hope you know that you're an inspiration," an older lady says, her face filled with joy. "My grandson told me you gave him the courage to come out. I've never seen him happier."

My heart fills with pride as I beam at her.

Stories like that are one of the main reasons I chose to come out last year. That, and I was sick of acting like my boyfriends were *just friends*. I've been out to my family since I was fifteen, but by then, I was already on my journey into country music. It would be a lot harder to make a name for myself if I was out and proud, so I kept the closet door shut.

Our band has been at the top of the charts for a while now, and with the blessing of my band members, we decided it was time for me to come out. The guys were strong enough to find a new lead singer if my coming out had crashed my career, but thankfully, it didn't. Although I'd give up all the fame now, knowing what it's like not to be hiding anymore.

Last year, when I made the announcement, a weight was lifted off my shoulders. As expected, we were met with some backlash, but overall, our fans supported us. It helped that our music was never *bro-country*. We didn't sing about girls climbing into our trucks or being some macho guys. I always wanted our music to be authentic, and singing about stuff like that was never going to work for us.

"Does your grandson have our newest album?" I ask the lady.

"Yes. He has everything you've ever put out. He's a big fan."

"Fantastic. What's your name?"

"Gladys," she tells me with a megawatt smile.

I wave Aria over. "Can you take down Gladys's information? I'd like to gift her and her grandson front-row passes the next time we're in town."

Gladys gasps, and tears well in her eyes. "That would mean the world to him. We couldn't afford to get tickets for tonight's show, but I was hoping that by standing out here, I could get you to sign this poster for him."

"And what's his name?" I ask, taking the poster and pen from her outstretched hands.

"Connor."

I autograph the poster with a flare, then move on to sign a few more things while Aria gets Gladys's information.

"Could you sign my arm?" a short man with wild, curly hair shouts. "I want to get your autograph tattooed on me."

"Wow, a *really* dedicated fan," I say. "Would you like the rest of the guys' too?"

He shakes his head. "No, just yours."

As I go to grab the marker from his hand, something pricks me, and I gasp, pulling away as fast as possible.

"What the fuck?" I yell.

"Are you okay?" Brando asks, his brows pulled together with concern as he turns to a security guard.

The fan who pricked me quickly steps back, looking worried but also apologetic. "Shit, sorry, I forgot my pin was in my hand," he says, showing a little rainbow pin. "I wanted to give it to you. Now I feel like a fool."

His lower lip trembles, and I feel like a dick, so I wave off my friend and the security guard, who are watching closely, and plaster on my best smile. "It's okay. Accidents happen," I reassure him, securing the pin to my jacket.

With the marker in my hand, I sign the man's forearm, then it's time for us to head to the hotel. The ride is uneventful and short, but by the time we arrive, I'm more tired than I should be. I usually hit the hotel bar for a nightcap after shows, but I'm wondering if I should skip that tonight.

"Anyone joining me for a drink?" Joseph asks as we walk through the hotel lobby.

When the other guys shake their heads, I cave, not wanting Joseph to be alone.

"Why not?" I say, even though my legs are a little wobbly.

We get situated at a table, and seconds after we order our drinks, a pretty woman struts over to us. "Are you Joseph Montgomery?" she asks my friend, who puts on a charming smirk.

"I am. What's yer name, darlin'?" he questions, putting on his southern drawl extra thick.

"I'm Patsy."

Joseph pulls out the chair next to him, gesturing for her to sit. "Well, Patsy, why don't you have a seat and tell me about yourself?"

With a knowing expression on my face, I push out my chair. "I'm gonna head to the bar while you two get acquainted," I tell them.

Joseph mouths *thank you* as I walk away.

I make my way to the bar, but my feet are heavy and drag with each step. My head is swimming, and I have to brace myself against a bar stool when I get there.

"You don't look so good," the bartender tells me as my head spins.

"I'm f-f-fi-ine," I slur, blinking fast, trying to keep my heavy lids open.

"I don't think you are," the bartender says.

Someone sits next to me, and when I turn my head, I'm face to face with the man who poked me with the pin at the event.

"J-Jo-Joseph," I call out before falling over, and the world goes dark.

Chapter Two

ARCHER

A BEEPING NOISE WAKES me. It takes an insane amount of effort to open my eyes. *When did my eyelids start weighing five hundred pounds?*

It feels like hours before I'm actually able to see where I am, but it was probably only a few seconds. I gasp when I realize I'm in a hospital room.

"What the fuck?" I rasp out.

Aria grabs my hand, and it's evident she's been crying by her tearstained face.

"Why am I here?" I ask.

"Let me get the doctor. He'll be able to explain better," she tells me, then rushes out of the room.

"Thank fuck you aren't dead," Joseph says with bloodshot eyes. "When you fell over at the bar, I thought for sure you were having a medical emergency or something. It scared the shit out of me."

"What actually happened?"

"I can give you that information," a man in a white lab coat, who I'm presuming is my doctor, tells me. "I'm Dr. Henderson. I've been monitoring your situation since you arrived. I'm sorry to tell you that you were drugged."

My eyebrows shoot up, the truth like a punch to the gut. *Who the hell would drug me, and why?*

"How did that happen?" I ask, more than a little confused. It's not like I had any unattended drinks.

"I believe the fan who pricked you with the pin last night is to blame," Dr. Henderson explains. "It's the newest version of needle spiking, and while we don't see a lot of it around here, it's been on the rise. Especially with the new drug on the market, Halinexus. Before, needle spiking had to be done with an actual needle, and the person would be injected without their knowledge. But with Halinexus, it's possible to coat any sharp object with the drug and prick someone with it. The smallest amount can make someone become disorientated and have trouble walking."

My eyes widen with this information and learning someone has used this drug on me.

The doctor continues. "Being that it is such a strong drug, it's extremely easy to get the wrong dose. You're lucky it didn't kill you. Some other people haven't been so lucky. Halinexus is the new drug of choice for people wanting to take advantage of others. This is the first time I've heard of the drug being used on a celebrity, but it makes sense. The fan is likely more than a little obsessed with you and was hoping you would leave with him by getting your guard down."

I shake my head and grab the back of my neck. *How the hell is this happening?*

"Please tell me you caught this asshole," I say to Joseph, who shakes his head.

"Sorry, man, I wish I did, but my attention was on you dropping like a fly out of nowhere. The cops are looking for him, but so far, he's disappeared."

"When do I get to go home?" I ask the doctor.

"We're going to keep you for a bit longer. We'll continue to pump you full of fluids and some antibiotics to make sure you don't have an infection and that there are no traces of the drug left. We will need to run another blood panel to ensure everything is where it should be before we discharge you."

"Thank you for everything," I murmur.

He smiles, placing his hand on my shoulder. "We are doing everything in our power to get you back to your healthy self. Take this time to rest."

"I will," I assure him, and he leaves.

"We've moved our flight to tomorrow morning to give you time to rest," Aria tells me, her voice distant.

I flip my hand, wiggling my fingers at her, and she grabs it.

"Are you okay?" I ask her.

She shakes her head as new tears pool in her eyes. "I was so scared," she whispers, her voice breaking.

"I'm sorry I put you through this."

She blinks away her tears and squeezes my hand. "You have nothing to be sorry for. But we need to hire full-time security. I'm not risking your life like that again."

I want to fight her because the idea of someone following me around all the time makes my skin crawl, but the look on her face right now isn't something I can argue with. She's terrified and hurt. If hiring a shadow will put her mind at ease, I'll do it.

"Hire whoever you think is best," I tell her.

Her lips pull up at the corners, and her shoulders soften at my words, assuring me I made the right decision.

I'm positive tonight was a one-off, but it's always better to be safe than sorry, right?

Chapter Three

BENNETT

AFTER ENTERING NIXON'S OFFICE, he hands me a file. I look it over, aware that he's waiting for a response.

Name: *Archer Dawson*
Age: *Thirty years old*
Relationship status: *Single*
Occupation: *Country Musician*
Born and raised in Los Angeles
Parents: *Timothy and Chantel Dawson. Married*
Siblings: *Three—Aria, Clayton, and Stefanie*
Twin sister, Aria, is band manager.
Reason for application: *Was drugged at last show by crazed fan. Potential stalker.*
What client is looking for: *A permanent team for entire band while touring and for events, and a full-time bodyguard for Archer.*

"Are we taking this job?" I ask when I'm done reading the file.

"I'm considering it, but these clients deserve the best we have to offer. They are high-profile clientele. One wrong move on our part could be the complete downfall of this company," Nixon states, a little more doom and gloom than normal, but he isn't wrong. "Which is why I will only take this job on if you agree to be the lead on the team and Archer's full-time bodyguard."

My brows shoot up. "Are you serious?"

"Of course I am. You know you're one of my number ones. I trust you with my life. This position is perfect for you."

I'm honored by the offer, and he isn't wrong. I would totally nail a position like this, and I've been craving a full-time role for some time now.

"Can I choose my team?" I ask.

Everyone who works for Hunter Security is amazing, but I work better with some than others.

"Absolutely. I've already drawn up a list of available people," he tells me, leaning over his desk to hand me the piece of paper and a highlighter. "Pick your team of five."

I look over the list and make my first three picks. The last two are a bit harder since I'm trying to keep in mind how everyone gets along with each other, but eventually, I have my team picked.

"Archer and his sister are coming in today for a meeting. You'll get to meet them at three o'clock," Nixon informs me. "Let your team know they've been chosen in the meantime."

"You already have a meeting lined up?" I question with a raised brow. "What would you have done if I said no?"

"I knew you wouldn't, but had aliens taken over your body, and if you *did* say no, I would have told them we weren't the right fit."

I laugh, pushing back my chair to stand. "Good thing no aliens have taken over my body today. I'll see you at three."

The clicking of heels and other heavy footsteps alert me that people are approaching the conference room. I glance up from my computer as a tall, handsome man, who I assume to be Archer, enters the room. A much more petite woman is by his side, followed by Nixon.

At six foot two, I thought I was decently tall, but here I am being proven wrong again.

Standing, I plaster on a smile and reach out to Archer, who looks fantastic in dark wash jeans that cling to his thick thighs and a tight black T-shirt that shows he works out often. There's something about a fit man, not to mention his beard.

"It's nice to meet you," I say, offering my hand. He takes it, and I hope he doesn't see how distracted I am as I take him in. "I'm Bennett."

His palm is warm, and the calluses of his fingers tickle the back of my hand as we shake. He stares at me for a moment, his blue-green eyes almost peering into my soul, causing my heart to race. But as I'm trying to figure out what is going on in his head, he blinks rapidly, shakes his head like he's caught off guard by something, and drops my hand like it suddenly burned him.

"I'm Archer, but I bet you already know that," he says, then gestures to the woman at his side. "This is Aria, my sister and band manager, and the reason we are here today."

She rolls her eyes and shakes my hand. "It's nice to meet you. I'm not the *reason* we are here today. I'm just smarter than my brother and take threats seriously."

As we all take a seat, I say, "It's smart to err on the side of caution. Being drugged isn't a joke."

Archer runs a hand through his well-groomed beard, and my eyes track the movement. *What would it feel like to run my cheek along it?*

Would it tickle my lips if I kissed him? Shit, I shouldn't be thinking like that. He's a client, not a bar pickup.

"You're right," Archer says, pulling me back to the conversation, where my head should be and not in some lust-filled daydream. "But it's still weird to me to have to hire a bodyguard. I didn't really think I was at that point in my career."

"I'm surprised you haven't needed security sooner," I admit. "Not just for obsessed fans but to deal with the possible backlash of coming out."

"We had temporary security around at that time, but the backlash wasn't as bad as we thought it was going to be. Another celebrity quickly took the heat off Archer," Aria supplies on behalf of her brother, but I keep an eye on him as she talks, wanting to know how this all makes him feel even if he won't tell me. "But things are different now. Country Skies has really blown up, and we are touring sold-out stadiums constantly. As lead singer, Archer is the front person for the band and has the most attention on him on and off the stage. It's in everyone's best interest to have our own security team now."

Archer keeps quiet. It's obvious by his body language that he doesn't agree with his sister. His arms are crossed against his broad chest, and he even rolls his eyes a little when his sister mentions him having most of the attention. It was subtle, and if I weren't paying as close attention as I am, I bet I would have missed it.

It's my job to be aware of everything, but I must admit that I'm tuned in to Archer more than I ever have been to any previous clients.

"Bennett is going to be the head of the team and Archer's personal bodyguard," Nixon supplies.

Aria smiles at this knowledge, but Archer's neutral expression holds strong. He isn't giving me much to work with. If he would look at me, I might be able to get a better read.

"Is it possible to get a copy of what the band is currently scheduled for event-wise?" I request. "I want to make sure the team is available."

"Yep. I'll send a PDF file. I'll also attach the link to sync the band's calendar to yours."

"That would be great," I tell her, then turn my attention to Archer. "As for your personal security, I will be on call for you twenty-four seven. Any time you leave your house, I am to be with you. While on tour, we can discuss sleeping arrangements, but it's usually best to book suites, and I'll sleep in the spare bedroom."

The idea of sleeping close to this gorgeous man is intriguing, and if he weren't a client, I'd think about inviting him into my bed, but I don't cross lines I shouldn't. Yet, if he did the inviting, I don't know if I would turn him down.

"Think of me as your shadow," I continue. "Where you go, I go. If, for whatever reason, I need to take a break, one of the other security members will fill in for me temporarily, but you will be aware of this well ahead of time. If you feel like I am not a proper fit for you, you can contact Nixon at any time, and I will step down with no hard feelings. This is about making you safe, and your feelings matter."

I hope he doesn't want another bodyguard, as I'd like to get to know this man who has me reacting like this to a client for the first time, but I would respect his wishes. I meant what I said. His feelings are what matter the most.

"Thank you," he whispers but doesn't meet my eyes, making it hard to decipher his emotions. *Is he acting aloof because he doesn't want to be here, or is there something more?*

"Who is your current security system with?" I check with Archer, who casts a glance at his sister.

"He has a cheap system right now, but Nixon was saying you offer something better."

I'm already aware they have had this conversation, but I don't want them to think we are making plans behind their backs.

"We do. Are you interested in switching to our in-house security system?"

"Yes," Aria says.

Archer sighs. "Whatever makes this one happy," he murmurs, gesturing to his sister.

"What are your plans for this afternoon?" I ask.

Archer doesn't immediately respond, so Aria speaks for him. "He has no plans today. Tomorrow, the band has rehearsal at Archer's place, so that might be a good time to introduce the team to everyone."

"That would be perfect. Would it be okay if Nixon and I came by this afternoon to install the new system?" I ask, my attention on Archer, but he keeps his gaze on the table.

"That should be fine," he responds quietly.

The man's walls are high, and I need to figure out how to get them down. Obviously, he doesn't see the need for security and a bodyguard but cares enough about his sister to push his feelings aside to make her happy.

"Is there anything else you want from your security team?" I inquire.

"I just want everyone to feel safe," he supplies.

"We'll make sure that everyone is as safe as possible," I assure him.

Chapter Four

ARCHER

A SLEEK BLACK SUV follows me on my drive home, which would be worrisome in any other circumstance. However, it's different this time because it's not a stranger behind me. It's my new bodyguard.

My bodyguard.

A man who is sex on legs and is causing my brain to short-circuit.

"Why were you so surly in there?" Aria asks as I try to focus on driving.

"I wasn't," I argue.

At least, I don't think I was. Even if I was, it's because I was thrown off when we entered the conference room. I'm not sure what I was expecting from my bodyguard, but it sure as hell wasn't Bennett—a tall man with broad shoulders, deep umber eyes, warm brown skin, and a voice so deep and smooth it sends shivers down my spine.

I'm around attractive people reasonably often in my career, but I was still taken back by how sexy he is. Most security guys I've worked with in the past all looked average, but I swear Bennett could be a model.

"Look, I know having a full-time bodyguard isn't something you really wanted, but Bennett seems like a nice guy." She pauses and sighs. "Can you just give him a chance?"

Oh, she thinks I'm acting off because I don't want a bodyguard.

That's better than her knowing the truth—that I'm ridiculously attracted to him. But how do I agree to give this man a chance when he makes me all hot and bothered? It's not like I'm constantly having to work closely with people I'm attracted to. Honestly, it's rare I'm this instantly attracted to *anyone*.

"I'll give him a chance," I assure her, praying I can push away this attraction.

It would be all kinds of wrong to mess around with my bodyguard, wouldn't it? Besides, I don't even know if he's into guys.

Turning my focus to the road again, I try to forget about the handsome bodyguard who is going to be a new permanent fixture in my life. It takes us about half an hour before we pull up to my acreage, and I put in the code to open the gates at the entrance of my driveway.

One of the reasons I didn't see the need for an expensive security system is my property is hard to access. Why would someone need some state-of-the-art system when their house is in the middle of nowhere?

I smile when my house comes into view, bringing the memories I've already made here to the surface. When I bought this property five years ago, the building that was originally here was in disarray, but I didn't care because I knew I wanted to start fresh. I wanted a place that felt like home every time I walked through the door, and I was able to make my dream come true. The five-bedroom, two-story modern farmhouse might be too simple for some people who live around here, but it's perfect for me. I don't need a mansion, and I hate flaunting my money.

Normally, I would park in my attached garage, but I decided against it since Bennett is here. I don't want to be rude and make him wait for me to walk out of my garage.

"Nice place you've got here," Bennett notes as he and Nixon walk over to Aria and me. He offers me a genuine smile that lights up his face and has my heart racing.

"Thanks," I reply, shoving my hands in my pockets. Aria shoots me a *be nice* look at my gesture, again thinking I'm being rude, when, in reality, I'm trying to hide how I feel about this man. "I know it's not a mansion, but it's home."

"What's that building over there?" Nixon asks, pointing toward the back end of my property.

"It's my recording studio. It's where practice will take place tomorrow."

Bennett writes something on a pad of paper that he brought with him. "Mind if we walk around for a minute?" Bennett asks, adding, "We'll meet with you after to go over a game plan for the security system."

"Take all the time you need. I'll pour us all some water and meet you on the back porch," I tell him, then Aria and I head inside.

"They are both super handsome," Aria whispers as we walk to the kitchen.

"I've noticed," I mumble.

My sister squeaks. "Is *that* why you're acting weird?" she questions, and I know I can't lie to her. "Because you think Bennett is hot?"

I sigh, rolling my eyes. "Maybe."

Aria laughs, shaking her head. "This is fantastic. But if it makes you too uncomfortable, we can ask Nixon to bring on someone else."

"No, Bennett seems like a good guy. I probably just need to get laid. I haven't been with anyone since Peter and I broke up six months ago. Clearly, I'm just horny and losing my head a bit."

Aria raises a brow, not convinced. "Whatever helps you sleep at night," she sing-songs, reaching for some glasses.

I help her fill them with ice and water, then carry them outside and wait for our guests. Then, when Bennet walks by, waving at us with his killer smile, my heart races.

How the hell am I going to be able to blow off steam with a new shadow?

Chapter Five

BENNETT

IT'S SIX O'CLOCK IN the evening by the time we have everything set up and connected to the servers. I'm surprised we worked as quickly as we did, especially with all the covert glances I kept stealing at Archer. I was trying my hardest not to stare at the sexy musician since I didn't want Nixon to pick up on my attraction, but it's hard not to. The man is fucking hot.

"Do you have any questions?" I ask Archer.

"Nah, this is all pretty straightforward. I'm still going to stand behind the fact that I think this is overkill, but it's pretty cool that I can see almost all of my property from the cameras," he tells me, and there is a hint of a smile on his lips.

What would it take to get a full grin out of him?

"It's just a precaution, but no one will be able to get on your property without us knowing now."

"What if I'm having a guest over?" he asks.

"Send me a text so I know the person was invited. Same thing goes if you get any deliveries."

"Okay," he mumbles, tipping his head in agreement.

"If you have any questions, reach out to me whenever. My phone will always be on. If you have even the slightest bit of unease, I'm here for you," I assure him, staring into his soulful blue-green eyes.

He holds my gaze longer than most would but eventually blinks like he did at the office and stares at the floor. "See you tomorrow," he murmurs, that wall I noticed in the office fully in place again.

"You bet," I reply casually, trying to make my voice cheery and bright, hating this uncomfortable space between us. He should feel confident and secure knowing I will keep him safe. That's something I'm going to have to work on.

When clients don't want a bodyguard, it makes my job harder. Often, they end up doing stupid shit because they think they are invincible and the precautions we've put in place aren't necessary. I hope Archer isn't one of those guys, and his love for his sister and band members is enough to keep him in line.

With Archer's approval of the system, Nixon and I say goodbye, then make our way back to the office to unload the unused equipment and for me to grab my car.

"Do you think Archer is going to be a challenge?" Nixon asks during the drive.

I tilt my head from side to side. "The possibility is there. He doesn't believe there is a threat against him, and he definitely doesn't want a full-time bodyguard. But it's evident that he cares for his sister and bandmates, so hopefully he takes things seriously."

Nixon hums his agreement. "What's your gut telling you about Archer's threat level?"

"It isn't happy," I admit. "There's the possibility that the drugging was a one-off, but something about that doesn't sit right with me, but I don't know why yet."

"Talk to Sophy," Nixon encourages me, mentioning the company's tech guru. "I already have her checking the footage of the hotel bar the night Archer was drugged to see if we can ID the guy, but maybe she can scrub Archer's social media accounts and fan emails to see if there are any concerning messages."

"I was thinking that too. I'm also going to ask Aria for Archer's physical fan mail."

"It might be a good idea to try and become friends with Archer too," he suggests. "People are often more at ease and willing to listen to people they trust. His sister obviously trusts our company, but he's not one hundred percent there yet."

"I'll work on it," I reassure him.

It's JUST AFTER NINE when I get home, and I'm brainstorming ideas on how to get Archer to trust me more when my phone dings in my pocket.

Aria: *Archer goes for a run every morning. I completely forgot to mention it, but he often runs off his property. I have a strong suspicion he isn't going to message you in the morning, even though I told him to.*

An image of Archer running with sweat dripping down his body pops into my head. Of course, in this daydream, he isn't wearing a shirt, and he's pouring a bottle of water over his head because he's too hot. My cock loves the idea and hardens behind my pants zipper.

Shit. I can't be thinking like this. It's so unprofessional. This has never been an issue for me in my years as a bodyguard.

Why is Archer different? Why do my thoughts keep going straight for the gutter regarding this man?

I give my head a shake and respond to Aria.

Me: *Thanks for the heads up. I'll send him a text now.*
Aria: *He might lie to you.*

I smirk because I was already thinking that would be the case. From the way Archer has been putting up barriers between us, it's easy to see that he isn't going to want to have too much one-on-one time with me quite yet. But it's my job, and I don't plan on failing at it.

Me: *I'm prepared for that. What time does he normally leave the house?*
Aria: *Anywhere between five and six. He's one of those awful morning people.*

I snicker because I'm *also* an awful morning person.

Me: *Sounds good. I'll make sure to be outside his property around that time.*
Aria: *You're the best!*

Exiting that text conversation, I create a new one for Archer.

Me: *I hear you like to run in the mornings.*

Archer doesn't respond right away, but I wasn't expecting him to. There is a strong chance he won't reply at all. So, instead of waiting around, I head to my bedroom and strip out of my clothes, ready for a hot shower to wash away the day.

As the water is warming, my phone dings, and I'm pleasantly surprised when Archer's name appears on my screen.

Archer: *I hear my sister has a big mouth.*

I chuckle, and a second text comes in before I have time to respond.

Archer: *I'll stay on my property tomorrow. No use you getting out of bed at the ass crack of dawn. I know most people hate mornings.*

A sudden pang of disappointment radiates in my chest at his rejection. I knew this lie was coming, yet for some reason, it hurt, but I won't let it deter me. I'll figure out a way to get him to let me in.

Acting like his message doesn't affect me, I reply.

Me: *Lucky for you, I'm also a morning person and love a good run.*

Another message doesn't immediately come through, but from the dots floating in the corner of the screen, it's obvious he's typing away, so I wait patiently for the excuse he's coming up with.

Archer: *I don't want to bother you.*
Me: *It won't be a bother, I promise. See you at five.*

The dots dance in the corner of my screen again but stop, and no other messages pop up. I'm not surprised in the least. I bet he's grumbling to himself about me not taking no for an answer. Or maybe he's calling his sister to bitch about her ratting him out. Either way, it's fine by me. The faster Archer realizes he isn't getting rid of me that easily, the better.

Obviously, I would like Archer to *want* me around for his safety, but I'll take acceptance for now.

Chapter Six

ARCHER

My sister is the worst sometimes. Okay, that's a harsh statement, considering she only wants what's best for me, but it's still annoying that she didn't trust me to tell Bennett about my morning runs. She was right not to trust me, but it's irritating, nonetheless.

I run the same paths all the time, and *nothing* has happened in the past. Why do I have to have a babysitter now? I get that the drugging was scary, but that was in a whole different state. The crazy fan isn't here. If he were, wouldn't he have tried something already?

I shake my head and tie my shoes when the buzzer on my gate goes off. I guess Bennett is one of those guys with the thought process that if you're not early, you are late because it's quarter to five.

With a sigh, I hit the button to let Bennett in and head outside to wait for my new shadow.

"Ready for a run?" Bennett asks after he gets out of his vehicle, making his way over to me.

I look up and nod, taking in how, even in basketball shorts and a plain T-shirt, he looks sexy as sin. His smile is bright, but his eyes are covered by a pair of black Ray-Bans. I hate when people wear sunglasses, even if they are practical, which they aren't right now, seeing as the sun is only starting to rise.

Eyes tell so much about a person. When they're covered, it's like they are hiding behind a fortress. Or maybe it's my control-freak ways hating that it makes it harder to read a person.

"Do you always wear sunglasses when it's dark out?" I question, wanting to be a smartass for the moment.

Bennett snickers, moving them to the top of his head so they rest on his raven hair. "I figured by the time our run was over, I might need them, but I'll take them off if they make you uncomfortable," he offers.

I lift my shoulders in a nonchalant way, acting like I don't care, even if I do.

Without me having to say a word, Bennett runs to his car, discards his sunglasses, then darts back to me. "What way do you like to run?" he asks.

Instantly, I'm worried I made a mistake by hinting that he take the sunglasses off. His soulful eyes are far too easy to get lost in.

"I take a couple of different paths, but I need a long run today," I tell him, then realize I've forgotten my water bottle. "Did you need a water?" I check, heading up the steps to my front door.

"Sure, I forgot to bring one this morning. I'll remember tomorrow."

Tomorrow. That's right, this is going to be a regular thing.

Inside, I reach into the refrigerator to grab two water bottles and make a resolution to stop acting like an ass. I'm not normally this big of a grump, and putting on a front is tiring as fuck. I'm stuck with Bennett, at least for a while. It's best that we become friends because there is no way I want to live with this awkward tension for months.

Once I'm outside again, I hand him a water bottle and say, "I normally do a soft jog for five minutes to warm up my muscles, then take a break for a stretch before really pushing it. Does that work for you?"

"Sounds great," he says with that bright smile I'm starting to think is a semipermanent fixture on his face. That's also when I notice his dimple, and I damn near swoon. *How is this man a bodyguard and not a model or something?*

"Perfect, let's get going, then."

Bennett follows me through my property to the back gate that leads us to a walking trail. I put in the code for the lock and hold it open for my bodyguard, who beams at me in response.

"Tell me a bit about yourself," I press as we jog through the trail system.

The air has a chill to it, but it's not too cold. It is the perfect temperature for running, at least in my opinion.

"I grew up in Nashville," he starts.

I raise a brow. "How come you don't have an accent?"

He chuckles. "I didn't particularly like it, so I worked hard to lose it. It comes out when I'm angry or drunk, though."

I titter. "That makes sense. I have a few friends like that." Not wanting things to become awkward, I ask, "Is your family still there?"

"Yup. My dad is a pastor at a small church. My momma is retired but watches my brother's three kids while he and his wife work."

Pastor?

Shit, I wonder if Bennett is homophobic.

"My parents are the nicest people you'll ever meet," he continues. "Not going to lie. I was a little nervous to come out a couple of years ago, but they accepted me with open arms. My dad isn't one of those pastors who thinks all gay people are going to hell. He says God judges us on what's in our hearts, not who we love."

I smile, the worry I was harboring melting away.

"So, you're gay?" I ask, wanting to make sure I wasn't hearing things, but he shakes his head.

"I think pansexual is the label that best describes me, but I also kind of hate labels, if I'm being honest."

"I get that. It's like being put into a box," I muse out loud.

"Exactly, but I also get why people like labels. It gives them a sense of identity. I'm kind of a *whatever floats your boat* kind of person."

I chuckle, then almost gasp when we arrive at the opening where I stretch. *Have we been jogging for five minutes already? Wow, time sure is flying.*

Maybe it's because Bennett is an intriguing man. But that doesn't totally add up. I've had many conversations with plenty of interesting people in the past, but none felt like this. There is a connection between Bennett and me that I've never experienced before.

"Ready to stretch?" I ask.

"Yep," he responds.

We're silent as we extend and move our now-warm muscles, making sure they don't get injured when we exert them. The quiet isn't awkward. It's actually comfortable. That is until I cast a glance at Bennett touching his toes. His perfect ass is high in the air, almost as if it's on display for me, and I have to avert my eyes because my cock is already chubbing in my shorts. The last thing I need is for my bodyguard to think I'm a pervert.

I close my eyes, take slow, deep breaths, and continue to stretch, trying my hardest to keep my thoughts away from the sexy man near me.

After a few controlled inhales and exhales, I finally have my body centered, and I'm no longer worried about Bennett catching me with a full-blown erection. The last thing I want is for him to quit because he's uncomfortable.

I'm enjoying getting to know him and wouldn't mind learning more.

The things I could...

"All warmed up?" Bennett inquires, distracting me from my train of thought.

I beam at him, trying not to be awkward but probably failing. "Yup. This trail system will lead us into a neighborhood that we can run through, and the road will eventually take us to the front of my house," I tell him. "It usually takes me about an hour."

"Lead the way," he replies with a sweep of his arm and that signature smile. I find it's something I could become addicted to if I'm not careful.

I take off at a decent pace, and as predicted, Bennett is right on my heels. If those muscles barely contained by his clothing are anything to go off of, I bet he's in just as good, if not better, shape than I am.

Just because someone lifts doesn't mean they are a runner, but my bodyguard isn't showing any signs of slowing down. For some reason, that makes me happy. I haven't had anyone to run with in a long time. None of my band members like to run as fast or as long as I do, and if you ever see Aria running, you better run too because something is chasing her.

As we move, I lose track of the world around me, my brain drifts to song ideas, and I let my feet carry me on the familiar path home. Running has always allowed me to let go of anything that's stressing me out and to recenter myself. It's in moments like this that the best lyrics hit me. This and in the shower.

After we round a corner, a tune pops into my head, and I hum, wanting to keep the melody alive until I have a moment to pause and record it on my phone for later.

By the time we arrive at my front gate, my legs feel like Jell-O, and my lungs burn, but I'm still humming my tune with a smile on my face.

"What song have you been humming?" Bennett asks as I put in the code to open the gate for us.

"It's not a song yet, just an idea," I tell him, unscrewing the cap of my water bottle and taking a swig. A few drops miss my mouth and dribble down my chin, and I lift my shirt to use the hem to wipe away the mess. "I didn't want to forget it. That's why I've been humming it."

When I look at Bennett, his eyes are a deeper hue, and his signature smile is missing. If I didn't know better, I would say the look was lust-filled and hungry, but that can't be right.

He blinks a few times, then beams at me, the odd look replaced with a friendlier one. "That's a good idea. I'm also super impressed that you hummed so evenly as you ran."

Not wanting to think too much about what just happened, I begin the trek up my long driveway.

"How often do you get back to Nashville?" I ask while we walk.

"Not as often as I'd like, but usually twice a year. I wasn't planning on moving away from home, but I met Nixon when I left the Army, and he offered me a job here. I was nervous to take it, but it turned out to be amazing. I've really grown as a person being away from my family. You're from LA, right?"

"Yup, born and raised. Aria is my twin, and we have two younger siblings, Clayton and Stefanie. Our parents live in a nice gated community on the other side of town. I love my family to bits, but I needed some space, so I bought this property."

Bennett throws his head back and lets out a full belly laugh. It is deep and warm and brings a smile to my face. "I know that feeling. It's why I haven't really considered moving back to Nashville. I'd like to visit a bit more often, but I'm pretty sure I'd go insane if I were with them all the time."

"You've got an overbearing mom too?" I tease.

"Oh yes. In the best way, but I'm sure I would hear a lot more about how I need to find myself a partner if I lived closer. As it is, I already get a weekly phone call."

I chuckle. "I know the feeling. My mom keeps harping on me that music can't keep my bed warm or fill my house with laughter."

"Sounds like something my mom would say."

I down the rest of my water before we reach the front door, and so does Bennett. "Would you like another one?" I ask with a tilt of my head.

"Sure," he replies, following me into my house.

Instead of wasting water bottles, I grab two glasses and fill each with ice and cold water from my refrigerator.

"Thanks," Bennett says as I hand him the glass.

My fingers brush against his, and I suck in a quick breath. Tingles shoot up my arms, leaving me frozen for a moment.

Deep umber eyes meet mine, and that hungry look is on his face again, but he doesn't try to cool it this time. Like magnets being attracted to each other, we lean in, but before our lips can meet, my phone blares, and I jump back.

"It's my sister," I murmur, running a hand over my face, then grab my phone. "Is there something I can help you with?" My tone is filled with snark, but Aria is used to my attitude.

"Mom fell. She's in the hospital. Can you meet me there?" she asks.

My blood runs cold. "Is she okay?" I check with a lump in my throat.

"I'm not sure. No one is giving me much information," she grumbles.

"Is Dad with her?"

"Yes, but his phone is dead," she snips out, and I sigh. Our dad is notorious for not charging his phone. "Clayton is the one who called me, but you know how he is at relaying information."

Clayton is the youngest of us and is extremely forgetful. He tries his best, but if he doesn't write something down, consider that information gone.

There is no point in asking about our sister, Stefanie, since she's currently in Canada filming a movie. She probably hasn't even been told Mom fell yet. I doubt anyone will tell her anything until we have all the details.

"Okay, I'm on my way," I assure her, then hang up. "Can you drive me to the hospital?" I ask Bennett, who must be confused as to what's going on. "My mom fell, but that's the only information I have right now."

"Let's go," he says, placing his hand on my back and ushering me out the door.

His touch is warm and comforting, and I'm dying to lean into it, but I don't because that would be weird and wrong. Right?

"Are you okay?" Bennett checks as he drives, giving me a quick glance.

"I think so," I reply, a numbness taking over my body.

He nods but doesn't say anything else, and the silence is deafening for some reason.

"I'm scared," I admit. "I'm sure it's nothing, but what if it isn't? What if she's seriously hurt? I can't lose my mom." Tears pool in my eyes. I try to blink them away, but a few escape, cascading down my face.

Bennett reaches across the console and places his hand on mine but doesn't say anything because there isn't much to say. Instead, he's offering me strength through his touch. Without thinking much about it, I turn my palm over to hold his hand, and he squeezes, not letting go.

When was the last time someone offered me silent assurance like this? Has anyone just known I needed support and given it to me without question?

I don't even think my ex was this in tune with me before. I appreciate that Bennett is paying close enough attention to realize how affected I am right now and is willing to hold my hand as I break down inside.

The rest of the drive is quiet, but Bennett doesn't let go of my hand the entire time. Even though I'm still anxious, his touch is helping me from completely losing my shit.

After arriving at the hospital, Bennett follows me as I rush to the front desk. I miss his touch, which is weird and not something I have time to comprehend right now. I barely know this guy, yet I crave his touch. That's not normal.

"I'm looking for Chantel Dawson. I'm her son," I tell the lady at the front desk as my twin comes rushing into the hospital.

"How did you beat me?" Aria asks through panted breaths.

"I've got a fast driver," I say with a tilt of my head toward Bennett.

"Your mom is in room three-o-four," the lady tells us, and we rush to find our mom.

A pillow flies through the air as we enter the room, hitting Clayton in the face. "I just broke my ankle. You don't need to treat me like a child," Mom scolds him. When she sees us, she sighs. "Great, you let everyone know."

"What happened?" I question as we make our way farther into the room.

"I tripped and fell down the stairs, but I'm fine," she assures me. "Your father and brother are overreacting."

"You're not as young as you once were, Chantel," my dad tells her. "And when you hit your head, it was scary. I'm sorry that I thought the worst, but it could have been something serious. So I'm not sorry about bringing you in. Besides, you *did* break your ankle, so stop acting like it was nothing."

My mom rolls her eyes but doesn't complain anymore.

"We are glad it wasn't something more serious," Aria says, grabbing Mom's hand.

"You two didn't have to come visit. I'll be going home soon," Mom states, but Aria and I shake our heads.

"Doesn't matter if it was even just a sprain, we would be here," I tell her. "You're our mom, and we want to be here for you."

"I have the best children," Mom says. "But now I have to know who this handsome man is standing behind you, Archer."

I startle. Shit, I completely forgot about Bennett for a second.

"That's Bennett," Aria introduces him. "Archer's bodyguard."

"Thank you for looking out for my boy," Mom tells Bennett.

He flashes her a smile. "Not a problem at all. I'm just getting to know him, but he seems like a pretty great guy," Bennett offers but is looking at me as he says it.

"He is. All of my children are amazing," Mom boasts. "Now that everyone knows I'm fine, would you please leave me alone to rest in peace?"

I titter, moving to hug her and kiss her forehead. When I move to pull away, she grabs me back in for a fierce hug. "You should ask your bodyguard out," she whispers in my ear.

I shake my head, and this time she lets me go. "I love you too, Mom," I reply instead of telling her that asking Bennett out would be a bad idea.

"Ready to go?" he asks.

"Yep," I answer.

The way he smiles at me has my heart racing a little.

Would asking Bennet out really be the worst thing?

Chapter Seven

BENNETT

THE DRIVE TO ARCHER'S place is quiet and awkward. We shared a moment but haven't had a chance to talk about it. I'm not sure if I'm supposed to bring it up. It's eating at me, but since Archer is my client, it feels wrong to talk about it unless he starts the conversation.

"Your mom is a firecracker," I note, wanting the quiet to end.

"She really is," Archer replies, smiling. "I'm glad she only has minor injuries."

"I'm surprised no one said that in a text."

"Dad never charges his phone, and Clayton isn't very good at relaying messages. I bet Dad told him to let Aria know that Mom fell, so that's what he did. He didn't think to add that she's okay," Archer explains, and I love how at ease he is with opening up to me. "He's a concrete thinker. Everything is very black and white to him. He didn't technically do anything wrong. He did as he was told. No one can expect him to do more than that when you know how his brain works."

I nod along with understanding. "I worked with a guy like that once. Sometimes, our higher-ups had a problem with it, but it wasn't like they could let him go. As you said, he didn't do anything wrong. People just had to come to terms with the fact that sometimes they needed to word things differently around him."

Archer beams at me, filling my heart with this serene warmth I've never experienced before. "That's exactly Clayton. He excels in some areas but struggles in others. It's obvious he's a little different at times, like when he struggles to understand certain social cues. But being the same as everyone else is overrated."

"Now, the only member of your family I haven't met is Stefanie."

"She travels a lot. She's in Canada right now filming the newest season of the drama series she's been on for the last four years."

"Oh, that's right. Isn't that the show about the hockey team?"

"Yeah, it is. It's crazy because I'm pretty sure that is not how real-life hockey works at all, but people gobble it up. She was nominated for an Emmy last year. I'm so proud of her," he boasts with genuine joy written all over his face.

"I bet. It's crazy that you have a country superstar and an Emmy-nominated actress in one family," I remark, impressed.

"Don't forget a fantastic band manager and a graphic designer," he adds.

I love that he holds all of his siblings to the same level. It's obvious family is important to him, which makes me like him even more.

"Sorry that this morning turned out to be crazy," Archer apologizes when I pull into his driveway.

"Everyone loves a little action now and then," I reply, trying to assure him I'm not bothered.

We sit silently for a moment as if neither of us knows what to say. It's Archer who finally breaks the silence.

"Do you have a change of clothes with you?" he asks, and I nod, but I'm not sure what he's implying. "I was just thinking that maybe you'd want to have a shower here. That way, you won't be late for the band meeting. Who knows what traffic is going to be like?"

I smirk because the meeting isn't for another four hours, and I'm positive I'd have plenty of time to run home and get ready, but if he wants me to stay, there's no way I'm leaving. I've never felt this close of a connection with someone in such a short time, and I want to continue getting to know Archer.

"I can make that work," I tell him, reaching into the back seat for my bag.

I always have at least two changes of clothes with me and an extra set of toiletries, just in case. Clearly, being overly prepared has paid off this time.

I follow Archer into his cozy house, and he shows me to a spare bedroom with an en suite.

"There are towels in the closet, and the shower is stocked with everything you could possibly need," he tells me.

"Bring home a lot of guys?" I tease with a smirk.

He scoffs. "Hardly. I'm far too busy for hookups. Besides, I'm more of a relationship kind of guy. I've never been one to play the field. I just like to keep extra stuff on hand in case any of my band members need a place to crash. I also have fruity stuff for Aria, but if that's more your jam, feel free to use it."

We stand silently for a few awkward seconds before Archer claps his hands and slowly backs away.

"I'm going to go shower too. I'll meet you in the living room when I'm done," he tells me, then rushes out of the room like the floor is on fire.

I shake my head, grabbing the back of my neck. We are playing a dangerous game here. Archer admitted he is a relationship guy, and I'm not. At least, I haven't been in a long time. Not since my ex ripped my heart out and left me a broken version of myself. If I don't tread carefully here, I could end up hurting him, which is the last thing I want to do.

It's been less than twenty-four hours since I've met the handsome country singer, but he's already growing on me. Obviously, there was the initial attraction. He's hot and knows it, but there is potential for something more between us if I let it. At least, I think so. We're compatible on a level I've never been with another person, not even my ex, who I thought I was going to marry.

I'm just not sure letting things grow would be a good idea.

ARCHER'S COUCH IS RIDICULOUSLY comfortable. I'm not sure I've ever sat on a piece of furniture as cozy as this one. It's like sitting on a cloud. My body instantly relaxes, and the longer I sit, the heavier my eyes get. I should move around before I fall asleep, yet I can't get myself to stand.

"That couch is a trap," Archer says out of nowhere, and my eyes snap open, blinking quickly as I try to get my bearings.

Did I actually fall asleep? Shit, that's not like me.

"It's too comfortable for its own good," I grumble, rubbing my eyes.

Archer laughs in agreement, moving to sit beside me. "I've fallen asleep on this thing more times than I'd like to admit."

"I can't remember the last time I've napped. It's really not like me," I tell him, stretching my arms above my head. I'm aware of the way Archer's eyes zero in on the flash of skin that appears from my raised shirt, but I don't say anything. "What time are you expecting the band?"

He shrugs, moving closer and licking his lips. "Shouldn't be for a while," he replies in a husky voice, still leaning into me.

The space between us is gradually disappearing. His lips are barely a whisper away, but right as I'm about to bridge the rest of the gap, the front door flies open, breaking the spell for the second time.

Maybe this is the universe telling me I need to stay away from Archer. While Hunter Security doesn't technically have a rule against sleeping with our clients, it's not exactly the most professional situation either. It's why most of us have our own personal rules against it. It happened once before and worked out for the couple, but I've never been that kind of guy. Things tend to get sticky, and while I can be replaced, it could still put a sour taste in the client's mouth for the company. I've never even thought about crossing the line before Archer.

"Mom is the most stubborn woman I have ever met," Aria bellows as she storms into the house.

"Clearly, you haven't met yourself," Archer retorts, earning him a glare from his twin.

When her eyes land on me, her brows shoot up, and she tilts her head to the side. "I wasn't expecting you to be here. I figured you'd drop off my annoying brother and get a few moments of peace and quiet before the meeting."

"Archer was worried about the traffic, so he offered me the use of his spare shower," I tell her.

"Oh, how nice of him," Aria responds dryly with a shit-eating grin.

She must sense there is an attraction between the two of us. Maybe it's a twin telepathy thing, or I need to do better at not being so obvious.

"What are *you* doing here so early?" Archer asks.

Aria lifts her shoulders. "Mom wouldn't let me follow her home, and I was bored."

"Since you're here, I've been meaning to ask if you have Archer's physical fan mail. I want to go through it and see if anything pops out as concerning," I address Aria, hoping to distract her from reading more into my being here already.

"Absolutely. We check the PO Box once a week and store the letters and parcels in one of the spare bedrooms until we get a chance to get around to them," she explains, leading me to the room. I gasp when I see a large amount of unopened mail.

"Don't act so shocked," Aria scolds me with a smirk. "We've been on tour and haven't had time to go through things in about a month."

"This is only a month's worth of fan mail?" I'm surprised my jaw isn't hanging to the floor.

"Country Skies is a popular band. This isn't *just* for Archer, but I bet a good ninety percent is."

I move farther into the room. "I guess I'll get to work. Care to help me since you're bored and all?" I ask, only half joking.

Aria giggles and plops herself onto the bed. "Get Archer to bring us some knives," she instructs.

I head to the living room to find Archer cuddled on the couch with a fluffy blanket, looking comfy and almost asleep.

"Where do you keep knives for opening boxes?" I whisper.

"In the island, the farthest drawer to the left," he responds, his eyes barely open.

Quietly, I grab the knives and make my way back to Aria, who is already going through the letters.

"Find anything fun yet?"

She sighs, holding up a burgundy thong. "Do you consider this fun?"

I chuckle and shake my head. "Who are those for?"

"Archer," she responds with a visible shiver.

"Doesn't everyone know he's gay?"

"Oh, these are from a guy. The note says, '*These are the same color as your guitar. Care to strum me the same way? Love, Matthew.*' "

A full belly laugh bubbles out of me, and I have to wipe tears away. "Does he get a lot of notes like that?"

Aria frowns. "Yes. It's very disturbing at times because he's my brother, but they're harmless. At least, I thought they were. Should I be thinking otherwise now?" she asks hesitantly, worry showing on her face.

"Not necessarily," I reassure her, hoping she doesn't feel bad for not thinking twice about the sexual letters. "You're right. Most of these are harmless, but how about we start sorting the notes by names? If we find a bunch from one person, that would be something to check out further."

Aria continues to go through the letters, reading each one out loud to me, stopping for giggle breaks between each one.

"This is so much more fun with a partner," Aria says as she sorts another letter into her pile, which she has organized by name in alphabetical order. "Archer doesn't like reading the smutty letters, so it's always been my job to sort out the heartfelt ones. If I trusted other people, I'd definitely delegate this task."

"I can take it over if you'd like," I offer, and her whole face lights up.

Even though I'm attracted to men and women, my body doesn't react to her like it does her brother. I quickly brush off the thought since I shouldn't be thinking about Archer like that, especially not while hanging out with his sister.

"That's really kind of you, but I don't mind sharing the job. At least I have someone to laugh with," she states.

I open another large box and pull out a coffee maker embossed with images of Country Skies' album covers. "This is cool," I say, turning it around to see all the designs.

"Some of these fans are far too talented. We'll have to put that in the recording studio."

I put it in the pile with the other homemade gifts, moving on to open another box. This one has a shadow box of dried roses and a note addressed to Archer.

I read it out loud, and an ice-cold shudder of unease races down my spine. *"I am yours, and you are mine. We will be together one day soon and then never apart again. X."*

"That's kind of creepy," Aria notes.

"Agreed. Do you have any letters from an X?" I question.

As she rifles through her pile, I look at the top of the box and sigh when I don't find a return address. There is a scan code, but all that will give me is the city it was sent from. I'll still get Sophy to check it out, but I'm not holding my breath that it will give me any useful information.

"Three," Aria says, pulling me from my thoughts and holding up the notes. "They didn't seem too weird, but now, with that gift, I'm not so sure."

I don't remember hearing anything that set off red flags.

"Can you reread them to me?"

"I love you, and your music has changed my life. X," she starts. *"Are you an angel? I've never met someone as perfect as you. X."* She pauses, searching a pile of drawings. "This was in the envelope with that note," she tells me, handing me a drawing of Archer with angel wings.

"The guy is talented," I state, but it doesn't erase this feeling of unease that has me in a tight grip and won't let go. "What's the last one say?"

"*I will love you until my last breath. X.*"

I pinch the bridge of my nose, trying to devise a plan. "Let's keep an eye out for any more items from X. I'm also going to let Nixon and Sophy know about this so that they keep an eye out on the social media pages."

"I'll let our social media manager know about them as well," she responds. "The more eyes, the better, right?"

"I like your way of thinking," I tell her with a forced smile, trying not to clue her in on my state of restlessness. "Now only like ten more boxes and what..." I pause, looking over the pile of letters in front of Aria. "Fifty more letters?"

Her lips turn up slightly, and she says, "Yep, that sounds about right."

"How 'bout you keep going through your pile, and I'll make my call? Then I'll be back to help with the rest in a few minutes."

"Sounds good. I'll just be here throwing up in my mouth while I do so," she tells me, but her smile is growing. Hopefully, that means she's not feeling as out of sorts as I am right now.

Pulling my phone from my pocket, I exit the room, lean against the hall wall, and dial.

"Hey, Benny-Boo, to what do I owe the pleasure of this call?" Sophy answers, and I chuckle.

"It's not exactly the most pleasant of reasons," I mutter.

She sighs. "Lay it on me."

"I've been going through Country Skies' fan mail with Aria, and we came across a name... well, more like a letter... that we need to be on the lookout for," I inform her. "Have you come across anyone going by the name of X in your skimming of the social media pages?"

The loud clicking of Sophy's keyboard rings through my ears as she does some searching. "I'm not seeing anything, but you wouldn't be able to make a username with just one letter. Let me do some more searching, and I'll call you if I find anything."

"Thanks, Soph. The letters seemed innocent at first, your typical *I love you, you changed my life* kind of stuff, but the present is what's concerning me. The letter attached was talking about being with Archer *forever*. I don't like language like that."

Sophy hisses. "Yeah, that's not good at all. Send me a picture of the label, and I'll figure out where the package was sent from. Maybe that will give us another clue as to what to look for. If you find anything more for me to go on, let me know."

"Will do."

"How'd the call go?" Aria asks when I enter the room.

"Not great, but Sophy is gonna try to find any accounts that might belong to X. It's hard with this person signing only one letter as their name. With the package, the only information she'll be able to get is the location it was sent from, which may or may not be helpful."

She nods, and I move to open more boxes. Thankfully, I don't come across any more surprises or ominous messages.

By the time I've finished helping Aria with the letters and gotten everything sorted away, she's back to her happy, chipper self, and some of that joy is making its way over to me. I'm still on high alert but not as anxious anymore.

"That couch is like a fucking siren for sleep," Aria notes when we walk into the living room to find Archer deep in dreamland.

"But it's so comfortable," I counter.

She giggles. "That's why he keeps it. It also helps when he's having bouts of insomnia."

"Does that happen often?"

She shrugs. "The band works weird hours. Sometimes, it's hard to come down from that adrenaline high. He also refuses any sleep aids because he doesn't like to cloud his mind. It's nothing to be concerned about, just life for traveling musicians."

I nod but make a mental note about it. I've had clients who like to leave the house when they have trouble sleeping, so it's good to be aware of something like this.

"Want a drink or something to eat?" Aria asks, walking into the kitchen. "The band will probably be here in an hour or so."

"I could eat. I only had a protein shake before our run."

Aria snickers. "I'm surprised you let my brother talk you into staying when you knew full well the traffic wouldn't be bad enough to keep from getting here on time."

There is a mischievous glint in her eye. She wants me to spill my guts, but I'm not that easy to crack.

"Archer asked me to stay. The reason behind why doesn't matter. My job is to make him feel safe. If that means hanging around until our scheduled meeting time, then so be it," I tell her with a carefree shrug.

She stares me down for a minute with what I think is supposed to be intimidation before her face lights up, and she beams at me. "I like you," she says, pointing her finger at me.

I titter. "Thanks, I like you too. Now, what are we having for lunch?"

She giggles and gets busy fluttering around the kitchen.

While Aria cooks, I lean against the island and stare at the back of the couch where Archer sleeps. I meant what I said about it being my job to make him feel safe, but it was a lie to say that was the reason I stayed. I stayed because I wanted to spend more time with the sexy musician.

Not only do I like Archer, but I'm attracted to him too.

It scares the hell out of me.

What am I going to do?

I have no idea.

Chapter Eight

ARCHER

My brain is foggy when I wake from my nap, but I'm well rested and ready to take on the world. I'll admit I didn't sleep the best last night. I was too worried about what the run this morning would be like, certain spending my morning with Bennett would be awkward. I didn't, however, have the slightest clue I would almost kiss him twice.

"Good morning, sleepyhead," Aria coos at me as I sit up and stretch my arms above my head, letting out a big yawn.

"Are you hungry?" Bennett asks, startling me a little.

I almost forgot he was still here. Or maybe I expected him to leave while I was napping. I'm not sure, but either way, his presence is a bit of a surprise.

Turning my head, I smile at my handsome bodyguard. "I'm starving, but I can get my own food."

"I've already made you a plate," he says, holding up a dish. Aria clears her throat, and a sheepish expression crosses his face. "Correction, Aria cooked, and I dished up your plate."

I chuckle and stand so I can make my way over to them. "I appreciate it," I tell them both. "How long was I out for?"

"A while," Bennett says. "You sleep like the dead."

"I'm pretty sure a tornado could rip through this house, and he wouldn't wake up," Aria remarks, and I shrug, picking up the chicken ranch wrap to take a bite. She's not wrong.

My taste buds explode as the food hits my tongue, and I consciously make sure I don't moan. Aria isn't a fancy cook, but whatever she makes always tastes *amazing*.

"What should I expect from this band meeting?" Bennett asks as I eat.

Aria is the best person to fill him in on that kind of information, so I let her answer.

"We're just going over schedules mostly, and I've got a few requests from the record label that I need to go over with everyone. Other than that, the guys might sit around and write a little, but it all depends on whether the music is flowing through them," she explains.

"Did you record that tune you were humming this morning?" Bennett asks.

I shake my head, but the melody pops back to mind at the mention, and I grab my phone to make a voice message. I'm used to recording music ideas like this, but having Bennett watch me so intently with admiration makes me nervous, which is weird. I'm *never* nervous about music.

"That's fun," Aria says once I'm done. "Got any lyric ideas yet?"

"A couple," I tell her, but don't divulge more. She doesn't need to know the lyric ideas are mushy and about brown soulful eyes I met only yesterday.

"Don't forget to write them down," my sister reminds me.

"I won't," I assure her.

It would be impossible to forget these lyrics as long as Bennett is around. Honestly, the more time I spend with him, the more lyrics pop into my head. *How would he feel knowing I'm mentally writing a song about him?*

A knock comes from the front door before Joseph walks in, happy as always. "Howdy folks, how's it going?" he greets us.

"Just recording a new melody," I tell him with a grin.

"Oh, I can't wait to hear it. I've got a couple of ideas floating around in my brain too."

It looks like we will be doing some writing once the meeting is over, after all. But how do I spit out the lyrics when Bennett is hanging around? I've never written a song about anyone while they've been there, and I've also never written a song about someone I'm into. Maybe Joseph's ideas will fit with my melody, and I can save my lyrics for another day. That would be ideal.

Landon and Brando show up a few minutes later, and we all head to the studio.

"This place is impressive," Bennett notes, taking in our special space.

The walls are a warm gray, and the floors are dark brown hardwood. We have black leather furniture arranged in a semicircle in front of the recording booth, and guitars hang all over the walls. A row of shelves run around on each wall, fairly high up, that house all of the awards we've won over the years, with plenty of room for more. Off to the side is a wet bar with a coffee station that gets used a lot when we have late-night writing sessions.

"What's that?" I ask Aria as she moves things around on the counter.

"It's a new coffee machine that a fan sent. It has all your cover albums and pictures from a few concerts all around it."

I take a step closer to examine it. It's beautiful. I'm often in awe of the talent some of our fans have, and I am positive I couldn't make something like this.

"That's so cool," Landon states, and I nod.

"Okay, enough *ooh*ing and *aw*ing over the new coffee machine. We have business we need to discuss," Aria shouts, clapping her hands to get our attention.

We grumble like it's some sort of chore, but there are smirks on our faces. We like giving Aria a hard time. She might be my sister by blood, but the whole band is like a family, so she's their sister by choice.

Aria talks, but I'm barely paying attention to what she's saying. I'm too busy casting glances at Bennett. I need to talk to him about our two almost kisses, but I'm terrified to do so. It's one thing to let my body take control and go with what feels good, but it is something entirely different to voice my feelings, especially when I'm not even that sure what they are.

I'm attracted to Bennett, and from what little I know about him, I like. If this were a different situation, I'd probably ask him out, but he's my bodyguard, and this is a sticky matter. But I am friends with my exes, so what's to say that couldn't be the same for Bennett and me? We could try something, and it wouldn't be a big deal if it didn't work out. We'd simply go back to how we were before.

"That all sound good?" Aria asks, and my eyebrows shoot up.

Shit, I wasn't paying attention to a thing she said.

When the rest of the guys nod, I join in, but Aria is looking at me with an expression that tells me she knows I wasn't listening.

"Okay, with that settled, why don't you guys get to writing?" she says but tilts her head at me before she walks outside.

"I'll be right back," I tell the guys.

"I'll get the coffee started," Brando states as I leave to find my sister.

"Want me to stay here?" Bennett asks when I get to the door.

"If you wouldn't mind. I'm not going far, but I'm pretty sure my sister is about to rip me a new one, and I'd prefer that to happen without witnesses."

He smiles with a dip of his chin. "I understand. I'll be here if you need anything."

"What's got your head in the clouds?" Aria asks the moment I'm outside. "You had a nap, so don't try to lie and tell me you're tired when I know you're not."

"I'm distracted," I admit.

Aria scoffs. "Obviously, but are you going to tell me *why*?"

"Bennett and I almost kissed twice, but you blocked it both times," I grumble.

My twin squeals and claps her hands. "That's amazing. You totally need to fuck him or let him fuck you. Whatever floats your boat."

With a glare, I hiss, "Could you keep it down?" Then I grab her hand so we aren't as close to the door Bennett is standing by. "I have no idea what I want to do. I'm sure sex with him would be great, but he's a permanent fixture in our lives right now. You're not supposed to shit where you eat."

She twists her mouth as she thinks about that. "I guess you're right. I'm just sick of seeing you lonely," she whispers.

"I'm not lonely," I argue.

It's not exactly a lie, but it doesn't feel like the whole truth, either. I'm not lonely because I have amazing friends and family surrounding me constantly, but at the same time, I would like to wrap myself around someone at the end of a long day. It would be different if I was only interested in sex. Sex is easy and mess-free, emotionally anyway. But I don't only want sex. I want a partner, and I'm not sure pursuing that with my bodyguard is a good idea. I don't even know if Bennett wants that at all. Maybe he simply wants a good time.

Why do things have to be so complicated?

"If you don't want to date your bodyguard, could I set you up with someone?" she asks.

I shake my head, glaring at her. "Hell no. I can find a date on my own."

"Why don't you, then?" she counters.

I sigh. It's stupidly hard to argue with someone who knows you so well.

"We've been busy. The band and music are my life right now. I don't have the time right now to put forth the effort relationships require."

She presses her lips together and huffs out a breath through her nose before finally conceding. I know she wants to say more, but I'm grateful she's dropping it for now.

"Want to give me the quick rundown of what I missed in there?" I ask, changing the subject.

"Honestly, it wasn't much. The label wants to add a few more dates to the upcoming tour so it will last until the end of the year instead of ending in October, and they also want you to release a new album at the beginning of next year. All stuff we already expected."

"Sounds good to me. We already have a lot of songs written and clearly more on the way. We'll just have to find time to record throughout the tour, which might be tricky."

"I'm already working on fitting that into your already busy schedule," she tells me with a smile.

"You're the best manager a band could ask for," I reply, offering her a toothy grin.

She giggles, pushing my shoulder. "I know," she sings, then skips back toward the studio.

I follow at a slower pace as a new melody pops into my head. It's not as fast as the one I was humming this morning. This one feels more romantic and actually suits the lyrics I've been thinking about.

I grab my phone and make a voice memo before joining the band.

For now, I think I'll keep this new song to myself.

Chapter Nine

BENNETT

My heart is racing, my breathing is heavy, and I'm covered in sweat by the time Archer and I get back to his house. I've always loved running, but I've been pushing my body harder than I usually do the past two mornings so I can keep up with the country singer, who is in better shape than I figured.

We still haven't talked about our two near kisses, and I don't want to be the one to bring it up. I have no idea what to say to him, even after thinking about it all night.

"Thanks for running with me," Archer tells me with a smile when we get to his front door.

"Any time," I respond. "Do you have any other plans for the day?"

He shakes his head. "Today is my day off, and I plan on relaxing. Maybe work on a few songs."

"Sounds like a decent day. I'm meeting with your sister and my team this afternoon to go over our plan for the upcoming tour."

"She told me about that. Maybe if I'm bored, I'll join," he says with a smirk.

I nod, not sure what else to say. The air is thick with an awkwardness I want to break but have no idea how to. Instead, I stand there like an idiot.

"I should go shower," Archer states, breaking the silence.

"Yeah, I should get going too," I reply, but neither of us moves.

Archer pulls his lower lip between his teeth, and all I want to do is kiss him, but we have to talk before I do that. Using all the resolve I have, I turn on my heels and head to my car without another word.

As I pull out of the driveway, I glance at Archer in my rearview mirror, still standing on his doorstep, staring at my car.

Should I have said goodbye? Does he think I'm an asshole for walking away like that? Am I overthinking everything?

I shake my head and focus on the road.

Dammit. I need to get my shit together.

MY SMILE IS FAKE as I wave goodbye to my team, and they shuffle out of the boardroom.

I hate to say I was disappointed Archer didn't show up, but I was. He had no reason or need to attend this meeting, but a small part of me wanted to see him again, even though I saw him this morning.

Yes, I know that's pathetic, but the feelings remain all the same.

"You're not very good at acting," Aria murmurs as she puts her laptop and tablet into a messenger bag.

"Um... what are you talking about?" I ask, blinking a few times, trying to make sense of her words.

She looks up at me, smirking. "That smile you've plastered on is the fakest one I have ever seen. Aren't bodyguards supposed to be a little less transparent?"

"I'm not transparent," I argue, but that makes Aria giggle and pat my shoulder.

"Whatever you need to tell yourself," she patronizes.

"If I'm so transparent, what do you think I'm hiding?" I question, crossing my arms over my chest and leaning against the wall.

Aria's eyes light up, and I have a sinking suspicion I'm not going to like her response. "Disappointment about what I haven't completely figured out yet, but if I was to put my money on anything, it would be that my brother isn't here."

Damn, she hit that right on the head. How the hell did she do it?

I don't respond immediately. Instead, I lift a shoulder, trying my hardest not to show my surprise at her accuracy.

"I'm not an idiot, Bennett. I'm actually very intuitive," she continues. "It's blatantly obvious that you're into my brother. He feels the same. What I don't understand is why both of you aren't acting on your feelings."

"It's complicated," I grumble.

Aria beams at me, and I want to kick myself for confirming her suspicions.

"You're worse than my meddling mother, you know that?"

Aria laughs and shrugs. "I don't care. I just want my brother to be happy. So, what's your game plan? Are you going to ask him out?"

I pinch the bridge of my nose, sensing a migraine coming on. I thought that by moving away from my family, I wouldn't have to worry about the meddling as much. Aria clearly hasn't heard about boundaries, or maybe she simply doesn't care because she is acting as if she's *my* sister. I pray no one at the office catches a whiff of this conversation because then the meddling will become a million times worse, along with a lot of jokes and some gloating.

My friend and coworker, Knox, was teased a lot about his complicated relationship when it started, and I may or may not have joined in on that. He even told me he hoped my next relationship was complicated so I could feel what he was going through. I was, of course, cocky, saying I'm not a relationship kind of guy. Looks like that is coming back to bite me in the ass. Who knew wishes like that came true? Not that what I have with Archer is a relationship.

"I don't have a game plan," I mutter after Aria pushes my shoulder and gives me a *come on* look. "We'll figure it out as we go, but I promise this won't affect how I do my job."

Aria sighs. "I'm sorry for being pushy. I only want to see my brother happy. I know that might not be you, but hopefully, someone will come along soon and sweep him off his feet. He deserves it."

She waves at me as she exits the boardroom, and a weight sits heavy in the pit of my stomach. Why does mentioning Archer with someone else make me want to throw up? I've known the guy for such a short time, and I'm already jealous at the mere idea of him being with someone else. That's not normal, is it?

If I continue to let these feelings fester without talking with Archer, I'm afraid it's going to affect how I do my job. So, with shaky fingers, I pull my phone out and text the man I can't stop thinking about.

Me: *You around? I'd like to talk.*
Archer: *Was thinking about going for a swim. Care to join me?*

My skin heats, and my cock chubs at the thought of Archer in only a pair of trunks, his body wet and glistening. Seeing him like that is going to make talking hard, but I can be strong. At least that's what I tell myself.

Me: *I'll be there in thirty.*
Archer: *I'll be waiting.*

With that, I clean up the boardroom and head to my house to grab swim trunks. Hopefully, by the time I get to Archer's house, I will have come up with an idea on how to have this conversation.

Chapter Ten

ARCHER

THE WATER IS COOL and refreshing as I dive under, plunging to the bottom of the pool and gliding across the length to the other side. When I come up for air, Bennett is standing there in a pair of trunks that are bright blue with black stripes. His deep golden brown washboard abs are on full display, and my tongue salivates, wanting to lick them.

His bright smile lights up his face, and I suddenly find it hard to talk. "Hi," I manage to get out eventually, my voice shaking a little.

Bennett chuckles and waves his hand as I pull myself out of the water to sit on the pool's edge and kick my feet. Bennett lowers himself beside me and puts his feet in the water.

"What did you want to talk about?" I ask after a moment of contented silence.

"Yesterday," he replies, staring out into my yard.

"About us almost kissing... twice?" I check, and he nods. "I wanted to bring it up this morning, but I didn't know what to say."

He chuckles. "Same. I want to start by saying I'm attracted to you, and just the little I know about you so far, I like... a lot." His words have me grinning, but I don't interrupt him. "I'm drawn to you in a way I've never been to anyone else, but I'm not sure I'm the right guy for you. I'm shit at relationships and haven't been in one in a long time. I don't want to be the guy who breaks your heart."

"I like you too, and I'm sure you're well aware of how hot you are," I say, gently pushing my shoulder into his, and the way he beams at me has my heart racing. "I feel the connection, the same as you do. As I told you yesterday, I'm a relationship guy, but I get that not everyone is. I want to note that just because you weren't good at relationships in the past doesn't mean you'll be doomed at them forever," I say, offering comfort and reassurance.

"I get that, but getting to know you yesterday was eye-opening. You're like this giant ray of sunshine, and if I ever dulled that, I'd hate myself," Bennett shares, his words like a blanket of warmth and comfort wrapping around me.

"You're sweet," I reply, and the tips of his ears turn a deep red as he blushes. "I don't want things to be awkward between us. I'd like us to be friends if that's possible." He nods, but his smile drops, and I wonder if I said something wrong. "Do you not want to be friends?"

Bennett gently kicks at the water but doesn't respond immediately. I don't want to push him, so I stay quiet.

"I want to be friends, but I think I want to be more too. I'm just scared," he whispers.

Wanting to comfort him, I place my hand on top of his. "It's okay to be scared." His smile comes back even though it doesn't quite reach his eyes. "How about we continue to get to know each other like anyone would in the dating phase and see how it goes? We don't have to put a label on things yet."

"I like that idea, but would I be able to kiss you while we get to know each other?"

I let out a startled laugh. "I think that can be arranged," I purr, leaning into him.

When his lips touch mine, goose bumps cover my body, and a low hum rumbles in my chest. *Has a first kiss ever been this electrifying?*

One hand gently caresses my face while the other grips my waist, urging me closer to him. I slide toward him, closing the space between us, and his tongue laps at my lips, looking for an invitation that I eagerly give.

As the kiss deepens, my cock hardens. All I want to do is jump into his lap and ride him, but we're not ready for that yet. Sex would make things too complicated right now, so I force myself to stay where I am and enjoy the kiss.

Bennett's lips are plush and warm, and his hands are surprisingly soft. He's taking control, but at the same time, he's gentle and comforting. He isn't pulling me onto his lap, demanding more than what I want to offer, and I appreciate that more than words can express.

When we finally break for air, both of us are panting and sporting boners that can't be hidden in these trunks.

"Want to stay for dinner?" I ask once my breathing has evened out a bit.

Bennett's face lights up, and he says, "I'd love that. Want to actually swim first?"

I laugh with a shrug. "I guess so. Want to play water soccer?"

"Sounds fun, but only if it's full contact," he replies, and the idea of his hands all over me as we play around in the pool sounds like an early birthday present to me.

"Absolutely." I stand to grab the nets so I can put them in place.

When Bennett notices what I'm doing, he gets up to help. Once we have them set up, we both jump into the pool, my handsome bodyguard making quite the entrance with his cannonball that has me laughing.

I was dreading having a conversation with him when he texted me earlier, but now I'm glad we got things out into the open. I will have to tell my sister about this soon, but right now, I'm going to have some fun with a guy I like.

With the ball in my hands, I stare Bennett down, his dark skin glistening with the water droplets clinging to his well-defined chest. He has a playful smirk on his full lips and a glint in his umber eyes.

"Ready to lose?" I taunt with a raised brow.

"I never lose," he replies, then lunges at me, reaching for the ball.

Before he can grab it, I pull it away and dive to my left, narrowly avoiding his touch. But as I move to get my feet back under myself, Bennett grabs me and steals the ball. Even though I put up a fight, there isn't much I can do to stop him. He throws the ball into the net with a strong arm and cheers at his goal.

"You got lucky," I grumble.

Bennett throws his head back laughing, and even though I'm down a point, a giant grin spreads across my lips. This is going to be a fun game.

Laughter fills the air as we play, touching each other much more than necessary. Caresses of skin here, groping of asses there, and full body grabs from time to time.

Bennett is so strong, and it's obvious I won't win the game fair and square, but I'm not above playing dirty. When he grabs me to steal the ball back, I lean into him and lick his neck, causing a shiver to run down his spine and for him to lose his grip on me. With my limited time and freedom, I toss the ball as hard as I can and yell at the top of my lungs when it lands in the net.

"Cheater," he mumbles, but his lips are still turned upward, so I know he isn't taking the game too seriously and is not upset by my little play.

We play around in the pool for a good hour, and by the time we get out, I've lost track of the score, and my cock is hard as a rock. I wish I could do something about it, but that will have to wait until I'm alone. I know if I asked Bennett to take care of me, he'd be all over it, but I have to stick to my no-sex rule for now.

When we get out of the pool, my phone buzzes across the table. *Who is calling me? If it's Aria, I'm not answering. She has blocked me enough already.*

After I grab two towels, I hand one to Bennett and wrap the other around my waist, walking to the table and picking up my phone. There are a few notifications, so I scroll through them.

Missed call from Mom and Dad.

Mom: *Sorry to bother you all, but I almost forgot your father's birthday tomorrow with all of this hullabaloo, and I don't want to forgo traditions because of a broken ankle. Would the three of you be able to put your heads together and plan a last-minute celebration for him?*

Missed call from Aria.

Aria: *I could cook something if Archer or Clayton can take Dad out.*

Clayton: *I'm working tomorrow, but I can come for dinner. I could even order a cake.*

Aria: *That works. Archer, can you take Dad out?*

Mom: *He must be busy. If Archer can't take your father out, I'll come up with a plan to get him out of the house.*

Aria: *Sounds good to me. I'll go shopping tonight and come over tomorrow afternoon.*

Mom: *Thank you all for helping. I wish I could do more, but I'm not supposed to put much pressure on this leg right now, and cooking with crutches is turning out to be more challenging than I thought.*

Clayton: *Listen to the doctors, please.*

Mom: *I'm trying.*

When I get to the bottom of the conversation, I shake my head with a smile on my face and glance up at Bennett.

"It's my dad's birthday, and it looks like I'm in charge of getting him out of the house tomorrow. Are you up for an adventure?"

"Got something in mind?" he questions, and I tip my head from side to side.

"Not really, but maybe we can brainstorm over dinner tonight."

"Sounds good to me. All I really need to know is what time I'm picking you up, but the more information you give me, the better prepared I can be."

I smile and shoot off a text to the group chat.

Me: *Sorry, I was swimming and didn't have my phone with me. What time do you want me to get Dad out of the house?*

Aria: *I want to have dinner ready for six, and I'll need at least an hour, probably two.*

Aria: *Oh! I also want to decorate so give me three hours.*

Me: *Okay, I'll come up with a plan and let y'all know, but I'll make sure he's for sure out of the house by three.*

Mom: *This is going to be such a good day! Thank you all.*

Clayton: *See y'all tomorrow.*

I put my phone down and strut over to Bennett.

"What would you like to eat?" I ask, placing my hands on his neck.

"Are you on the menu?" he inquires with a sinful smirk that has me feeling hot all over.

"Not tonight," I reply, having to force the words out because I want nothing more than for him to feast on me.

But I know myself, and if we throw sex into the equation, I'm going to think it's a full-blown relationship. It will hurt worse if Bennett decides he's not ready for that. There needs to be boundaries for the time being, even if they suck.

"Do you want us to cook or order in?"

"Order in. I'm not the greatest cook. That's why I have Aria," I joke.

He titters and pulls his phone out, scrolling to find us something to eat.

It's been a long time since I've hung out with someone other than my family or my band, and I have to admit it's nice. Bennett's company is soothing and something I could easily get used to, which is good since he will be around for a while.

Maybe if the universe decides to smile on me, he'll be around for a *long* time.

Chapter Eleven

BENNETT

Timothy and Chantel Dawson's home is located in a beautiful gated community, and it's obvious they take pride in their house.

Beneath each window on the first level of the front of the house are planter boxes with gorgeous flowers streaming out of them. The stone path that leads to the front door is lined with more flowers and greenery, giving this place a welcoming vibe.

While taking in the charming landscaping, I'm also keeping a close eye on Archer and our surroundings. It is my job, after all, to keep him safe. We might be growing something here, but that doesn't mean I can let my guard down, especially when we are out in public.

Once Archer's dad is ready, they make their way toward me.

"Nice to meet you again, Mr. Dawson," I say, shaking his hand.

He scoffs. "Call me Tim. Mr. Dawson is far too formal."

"Tim, it is," I reply, and we all get into my SUV.

"I'm sorry that everyone is busy today, and we can't do our normal family get-together for your birthday," Archer tells his dad, a playful glint in his eyes. "But I've got something super fun lined up for us."

"I don't need anything for my birthday, but I appreciate you wanting to spend time with your old man. I just hope your mother will be okay on her own."

"She'll be fine," Archer assures him.

Aria should be showing up at their house in about five minutes to get things ready for the birthday dinner and to make sure Chantel has someone around just in case.

"I know, but I worry about her. We aren't young pups anymore," Tim jokes.

"You look plenty young to me," I tell him.

His smile grows, but I see him waving me off through the rearview mirror. "You're only being nice because it's my birthday."

"I would never do that. I mean it. You're just as spry and handsome as your son."

When I look in the mirror again, Archer is smiling softly at me. It has me melting for him a little more. I have to play things carefully today because we aren't technically dating, but I also want to win his father over in case things progress, which I suspect they will.

I still have to tell Nixon about Archer and me. Even though he's my friend, he's still my boss and deserves to be filled in because this has a chance to also affect his business.

"Where are we?" Tim asks as we pull up to a large, plain building, and I put the car into park.

"Can't you read?" Archer teases his dad.

Tim squints at the writing on the side of the building, then his eyes go wide. "Axe throwing?"

"Yep," Archer says. "It's supposed to be lots of fun, and they assured me no one has lost any fingers at this location."

Tim laughs, giving his son a gentle push. "Don't you think I'm a little old for this?"

"There's no age limit, so you're good to go," Archer assures him.

Tim shrugs and opens the door. "Do you think your mother will kill me if I accidentally kill you?" he asks, and we all laugh at his joke.

When we get inside, we have to fill out a few forms. After that, a young guy gives us a demonstration on how things work and the best techniques before leaving us to enjoy ourselves.

"Your dad is good at this," I whisper to Archer a few minutes later, watching Tim throw another axe that lands perfectly in the bullseye.

With a giant smile on his face, Archer says, "He's making me feel bad. I still haven't hit the target."

I chuckle. "It's because your movements are too static. You need to loosen up, be more fluid. Watch me."

Tim moves out of the way so I can take my turn. I take a step before throwing the axe, and as it soars through the air, I watch and smile when it lands in the center of the target.

"You both make this look easier than it is," Archer grumbles.

"Practice makes perfect. Just keep trying," Tim encourages his son.

Archer sighs but takes the axe from me and tries again. This time, he's a lot closer, and when he turns around, his smile is so big I wonder if his jaw hurts.

"Did you see that?" he asks.

"A few more times, and you'll be hitting the center, I'm certain of it. Why don't you keep practicing while I take a break?" Tim suggests, moving to a table at the back of our lane.

I sit next to him, and we watch as Archer throws axe after axe.

"He's getting better," I note, and Tim dips his head in agreement.

"Thanks for looking out for my son," he tells me.

I shrug. "It's my job, and Archer makes it easy."

"I'm proud of all my kids, but both Archer and Stefanie give me extra gray hair with their career choices. Being in the public eye, like they are, is scary at times. It's nice to know that someone has my son's back."

"I'll always have his back for as long as I'm in his life," I assure him.

"I believe that," he says, looking at me with a comforting grin. "I'm a good judge of character, and I can tell you're a good person."

I smile and thank him before turning my attention back to his son. I've always been proud of the person I am, but I'm still not sure I am good enough for Archer. He deserves the best. But maybe if I'm able to push my fears aside, I *can* be that for him.

AFTER AXE THROWING, WE went to a microbrewery for a tour and a couple of drinks. Well, Archer and Tim drank. As the driver, I stayed sober, of course. We laughed and talked the entire time, and I was completely at ease.

Tim and Archer talk animatedly in the back seat of my SUV as I drive us back to the Dawson house, and it makes me miss my own family a little.

I should call my parents tonight.

Today has been a pretty great day. It has me wondering what it would be like to spend even more time with Archer and his family.

"Should I order us something for supper?" Tim questions when I pull into the driveway.

"Why don't we go inside and ask Mom first?" Archer suggests.

"You're joining us, right?" Tim checks with me.

"If you don't mind one more mouth to feed," I reply.

He scoffs. "Of course we don't. You're part of the family now, as far as I'm concerned. Anyone who looks out for one of us is always welcome here."

Archer beams at his dad, then looks at me with a soft expression I can't exactly decipher, but it makes me feel happy and cared for.

The moment we open the front door, Aria and Clayton jump out and yell "Surprise," causing Tim to grab his chest as he steps back.

"Are you trying to give me a heart attack on my birthday?" he asks with a stern tone that doesn't do much with how largely he is smiling.

"We've done a lot more scary things in the past. If you were gonna have a heart attack, you'd have had one by now," Aria teases.

"But I'm old now. Things don't work the same," Tim counters before hugging his daughter. He hugs Clayton next, then pats me on the shoulder. "I guess we don't have to order takeout, after all."

"Happy Birthday, Tim," I tell him.

"Thank you for helping us pull this off," Aria says.

"I didn't do anything except drive them around. You definitely don't have to thank me."

She rolls her eyes before walking away, and Archer chuckles. "I'm gonna have to tell her about us," he whispers.

"I have to tell Nixon too."

"I understand," he replies with that warm smile that makes my heart beat a little faster yet puts me at ease at the same time. "If you need me to sign anything, let me know. I get that you being my bodyguard puts us in a bit of an odd dynamic. I don't want to cause any trouble for you at work."

"There have been workplace relationships before, so it shouldn't be a big deal, but I'll ask Nixon if anything needs to be signed."

There is more that we should talk about, but now isn't the time. So, I follow Archer into the kitchen where the rest of his family is and join them for an entertaining evening of laughter, jokes, and many trips down memory lane. I'm honored to have been included in an evening like this. And even though I'm Archer's bodyguard, I'm being treated as a guest tonight, and it makes me happier than I thought it would.

The Dawson family welcomed me in today with open arms, and it has me thinking about a future with Archer, which seems less terrifying each time.

Chapter Twelve

ARCHER

My guitar hums as I strum it, filling my living room with a soft melody. I'm working on the song that's been plaguing my brain for the last couple of days while I wait for Aria to show up. We need to go over my schedule for the week, and I also have to tell her that Bennett and I are maybe... kind of... seeing each other, but also, not really at the same time. Saying it's complicated is an understatement.

Spending the day with him and my family yesterday was amazing. It has me praying that Bennett will want to move our relationship forward, but I refuse to push him. If he doesn't come to feel the same way as I do, I'll just have to accept that. I think it's mainly his fear holding him back, so hopefully, with time, he'll move past that.

I'm writing out some lyrics on a piece of paper when the front door opens, and Aria walks over to me.

"Whatcha working on?" she asks, plopping into the rocking chair.

"A song that keeps getting stuck in my head," I tell her, putting my pen down. "Since you're my twin *and* band manager, I figured you should know that Bennett and I have decided to be more than friends but not exactly in a relationship yet. We are playing it by ear and getting to know each other better, but there is the potential for it to build into more." My words come out fast, but it's better to rip off the Band-Aid.

Aria beams and claps her hands. "That's wonderful news. Have you kissed him yet?"

I roll my eyes, but I can't stop my lips from pulling up. "I don't kiss and tell," I lie.

"Bullshit, but I'll let you keep things to yourself for now," she grumbles.

"I appreciate it. So, what do we have on the schedule this week?"

"As the rest of the band knows, since they paid attention at the meeting..." she shoots me a menacing look, "... together, you have one TV appearance and a few radio interviews. Plus, I was able to schedule you some recording time this week, and I've already confirmed the date and time with Brando, Joseph, and Landon. Other than that, you'll have staging, final rehearsals, multiple full run-throughs... plus, the stylists need time for last-minute fittings and all the usual rigmarole that comes with a tour. I still can't believe this one starts in two weeks."

"Time is flying by," I reply. "But I love being on tour."

Nothing compares to being on stage, hearing the roar of the crowd, and feeding off the fans' energy. Tours allow me to experience that almost every night in different cities all over the world. There's also the added bonus of getting to meet fans from other places, and when they tell me how much my music means to them, it fills my heart with an extraordinary amount of joy.

"Might be even more fun with your boyfriend being there this time," she teases.

"He's *not* my boyfriend," I argue. "Not yet, anyway."

"I'm only giving you a hard time. Do what makes you happy."

I smile at her and pick my guitar back up. "Want to hear the song?"

She nods with a goofy grin, and I pluck away at the strings, singing the words from my heart. While I sing, I think about the man I wrote the song about and how he's already stolen a piece of my heart in only three days.

So much for keeping shit under control. At this point, it wouldn't even matter if I slept with him. I'm already falling, and I don't think there is anything I can do to stop it.

"That song is amazing," Aria cheers.

"You really think so?"

Her head bobs up and down, and her face is lit up with radiant joy. "Absolutely. You need to put that on the next album."

My heart warms at her praise. "I'll talk to the guys about it."

"They'd be fools not to want it."

"Okay, enough about me and the band. Let's talk about you." I pivot the conversation. "What's new in your life? You are so obsessed with my love life, but what about yours?"

She sighs. "My life is boring at the moment, and my focus is on the band right now. Eventually, I'll focus on myself, but seeing all of you happy makes me happy."

I shake my head and grab her hand. "Just because you're our band manager doesn't mean your entire focus should be on us. It's okay to focus on yourself. I want you to be happy too."

"I am happy," she assures me, staring intently into my eyes, and I don't see anything to distrust there.

Our twin bond is strong, and I would know if she were lying to me. At least, I think I would.

"Let's order dinner, then continue this catch-up session. Too often, I feel like our focus is on business, or yours is on me," I tease, giving her shoulder a playful shove. "I want to forget about all that tonight and just be siblings for a change."

Her face lights up, and we pick a place to order from.

For the rest of the night, I silently vow not to think about Bennett, or at least not until after Aria leaves. Because I'm sure he'll be in my thoughts when I close my eyes tonight. It's not like I can control what I dream about.

Chapter Thirteen

BENNETT

NIXON SMILES AS I enter his office and pull up a seat across from his desk.

"How is everything going?" he inquires.

"Good, but I wanted to talk to you about Archer."

His face falls. "Are things not working out?"

I shake my head. "Quite the opposite, actually," I start, grabbing the back of my neck. My palm turns damp from the sweat that's already forming there. "Archer and I have been talking about dating each other."

Nixon's brows shoot up, and he leans back in his chair. "I was not expecting you to say that."

I shrug. "I wasn't expecting it either. You're well aware that I don't date, but there is something different about Archer, and he feels the same way. I wanted to tell you because you're my boss."

"It does make things complicated, but I understand better than most that the heart wants what it wants," he says with a smirk.

Nixon's husband was his client before they started dating, so he gets it.

"I wouldn't even consider crossing the line if I didn't think Archer was special," I confess.

"I know that, and you did say 'dating,' not fooling around, so I take that to mean you're over your fear of relationships?"

I sigh. "I wish. Unfortunately, the fear is still there. I am, however, starting to believe Archer will be worth it. The more I get to know him, the more I like him and the less time I want to spend apart. It's nuts that it's only been a few days, but I'm already a little crazy about him. I've never experienced anything like this in my life."

"Do you think Archer would be okay with signing a couple of forms?" Nixon asks.

"Yes. He already brought that up himself."

"He's smart," Nixon replies. "How do you feel about the possibility of your relationship being the center of the gossip magazines?"

"I don't *love* it, but I understand it's a possibility, especially if we take our relationship public."

"I'll get the forms emailed to Archer. I hope things work out for you two. You deserve a special someone in your life," Nixon tells me.

"Thanks. Fingers crossed I don't fuck things up."

With a quick goodbye, I leave Nixon's office and head to my car, pulling out my phone once I'm behind the wheel.

Me: *Just told Nixon. Expect an email with some forms to sign.*
Archer: *I told Aria too.*
Archer: *Want to come over?*
Me: *I'm on my way.*

With a giant grin plastered on my face, I make my way to Archer's house. The anticipation of seeing him again has my body humming. I have to pay close attention to the speedometer as I drive, wanting to get there as fast as possible but also not wanting a speeding ticket.

"Hey, handsome," Archer greets me at the door when I arrive.

When my eyes land on him, this unfettered need to touch him takes over me, so I grab his waist and pull him into me. He gasps, but it comes out more like a squeak. It has me smiling because it's not often that such a large man makes a sound like that. Then, before he can say anything, I lower my lips to his and kiss him like I've wanted to since we parted after our run this morning.

The way Archer melts into me has my heart racing. It pushes out more of the fear I've let run my life for far too long.

"I could get used to a hello like that," Archer breathes out when we break the kiss.

I chuckle and grab his hand. "There are plenty more where that came from, but would you mind if we talked first?"

He tilts his head, gesturing toward the door, then pulls me through his house to the backyard, where we sit on the patio bench.

"What's on your mind?" he asks.

"I want to tell you a bit about my past," I inform him, gazing into his gorgeous blue-green eyes.

He nods, waiting for me to continue. His demeanor is warm and welcoming right now, but the softness of his eyes is almost too much for what I'm about to say, so I shift mine away. I stare out across the pool and take a deep breath, trying to center myself and find the right words. I haven't talked about my past in a long time and hate opening old wounds.

"About eight years ago, I was in a relationship. I was so in love. I thought I was going to spend the rest of my life with her. But as you are aware, my job takes me all over the world, and my hours are not predictable. That took a toll on things, and she began to pull away from me. I tried my hardest to fix things, to shower her with attention when I could, but whatever I did wasn't enough. She kept telling me that I was married to my job, even after I cut my hours and spent as much time with her as possible. I almost quit Hunter Protection to make things work."

I pause as the memories of it all come flooding back, ripping the old wound open and causing my chest to ache.

This is why I don't like talking about the past. It's not that I still love my ex, but wounds like that run deep, and even though I've moved on with my life, the hurt she caused has affected me a great deal.

Archer places his hand on mine, squeezing it. He has a soft smile on his lips, and his eyes are kind and caring, making this a little easier. "Take your time," he whispers.

I inhale deeply, hold it for a second, then release it slowly. "The day before her birthday, I was able to get a coworker to cover my shift, and I went out to buy her an expensive necklace she had been eyeing for a while. When I got home, she wasn't alone." My eyes burn, and my throat feels like it's coated in a thick jelly, making it hard to swallow. "I... I f-found her in our bed fucking another guy."

It has been eight years since we broke up, but talking about it again is making it hurt like it happened only yesterday.

"I'm so sorry," Archer says, his voice soft.

"I'm surprised I didn't throw up when I walked in on them. My heart was ripped from my chest at the sight, but what hurt worse were the words she said to me after." I pause again, my lips trembling and my fingers shaking. "Sh-she told me it was my fault. I wasn't around enough. I didn't do enough for her. She said I turned her into the person she became, and she hated herself but hated me more."

The tears finally break free, and I take in a staggered breath. "When I told her I wanted her out, she lost her mind. How she expected us to stay together is beyond me, but honestly, I almost forgave her. She kept saying that any relationship I ended up in would be the same. I nearly caved, but my brother made me pull my head out of my ass, and I kicked her out. Unfortunately, her words have stuck with me all this time."

Archer pulls me into his arms, rubbing my back and humming a soothing tune. "She was wrong to tell you that," he offers after holding me for a while. "The problem was never you. It was her. There were so many other choices she could have made along the way. Her cheating is entirely on her, not you. Trying to put the blame on you, even after you had changed so much of your life already, was her looking to blame someone other than herself.

"Thank you for telling me. I know that must have been hard to share. I appreciate you opening up more than I can say. It helps me understand you better, and I get why you're afraid of relationships," he whispers, still holding me.

"I don't *want* to be afraid anymore, though," I admit, pulling away a little to look into his eyes. "I know we said we'd play this by ear and see how things go, but that almost seems silly to me now. It feels like we are so far past that. I already know that I like you and want to build more with you. But I'll be honest in saying I might need some patience and encouragement if I start acting like an insecure idiot."

Archer's smile is bright, and it's like the sun breaking free after a rainy day. "Are you saying what I think you're saying?" he questions, and I swallow the nervous lump in my throat.

"I want to be your boyfriend if that's okay with you."

No more words are needed, and Archer doesn't disappoint when he smashes his lips to mine for a savage kiss.

The sadness sitting heavy on my chest only moments ago is washed away by the man who has already changed me for the better.

Chapter Fourteen

ARCHER

BENNETT'S TONGUE SLIDES INTO my mouth, and a moan bubbles up my throat, causing my cock to stiffen.

When he confessed why he has a fear of relationships, everything felt like it clicked into place. I was honored he felt comfortable enough with me to tell me the truth. And I was absolutely elated when he told me he wanted to push his fears away for me. I couldn't help but kiss him.

I was hoping that *eventually* Bennett would want to be my boyfriend, but I wasn't expecting it to happen so soon. Only two days ago, he was still too scared to make that commitment, but now, here he is, telling me he wants me.

My body desperately wants to jump his bones, but my head is telling me we need to take things slow right now. I need to know why he had the change of heart to make sure we are on the same page here.

"Can we slow things down for a minute?" I ask when we come up for air.

"Something on your mind?" he asks, and it's hard to ignore the heat burning in his gaze.

Bennett is very intuitive, so it's better to come out with it right away. And I have to say, it's something I appreciate.

"I was just curious as to why you've changed your mind?"

"The more time I spend with you, the less hold that old fear has on me," he explains, holding my hand and stroking the back of it with his thumb in a soothing motion. "I like you a lot. You're different than anyone I've ever met. You're special to me. And yes, I know that it's fast to feel this way about someone, but meeting you has been like finding a missing puzzle piece. We click, and I've never felt this way before.

"When I was talking with Nixon today, I didn't want to tell him that we were *maybe* seeing each other. I wanted to shout from the rooftops that you are my boyfriend. That's when it all clicked for me. I'm still scared that I'm going to fuck this up, but I want you, and you deserve more than someone who is on the fence. So, I'm willing to face my fears for the chance at something amazing with you."

My lips turn upward, and warmth radiates throughout my chest at his words. "You don't need more time?" I double-check, needing to be certain this isn't a spur-of-the-moment decision.

He shakes his head. "I'm yours if you'll have me. I'm excited to date you and to go on this relationship journey with you."

I give him a quick peck and smile against his lips. I haven't felt this kind of joy in a long time.

"What is going to be vital is for us to keep our communication flowing. We need to make sure we are on the same page and talk through things when fear creeps in. I've been told it isn't always easy to date a musician," I tell him, wanting to be as honest as possible.

"That's a good idea," Bennett agrees.

"What's your opinion on the public finding out about us?" I ask.

Bennett tilts his head from side to side. "I'd rather not be under the spotlight, but I understand that comes with your job, and I'm willing to do whatever you need me to."

I've had exes in the past who refused to go public with our relationship even after I came out, which stung. It felt like all the effort I put into coming out was for nothing, but Bennett isn't making me hide it if I don't want to.

"How about we run things by my sister and play it by ear?" I suggest. "I'd rather keep things on the down low for right now because once the media sets its target on you, it can be a bit exhausting. And it could make your job more difficult."

Bennett's face lights up. "I like that idea."

"But telling Aria can wait. This can't," I say, pulling him in for another kiss.

This time, I don't want to stop. I want him in my bed, his body on mine, and us tangled up in the sheets with sweat coating our bodies.

"My... room... now," I pant out when I pull back.

The sexy smirk on my man's face has my cock throbbing. I didn't think it was possible to get any harder than I already am, but I guess it is, and I need to relieve the pressure as soon as possible.

"Are you a top or bottom?" I ask when we get to my room. I'm verse, so I'm not worried about his answer derailing things.

"I'm verse," he answers, and the sexiest thought of flip fucking pops into my head.

"Me too," I reply, licking my lips. "As much as I want to be buried balls deep inside you, I'm also desperate to have you wreck me. Will you fuck me?"

Bennett's eyes darken, and he bites his lower lip as he stares at me like he wants to devour me. Without breaking eye contact, he places his index fingers into the loops of my jeans and pulls me into him hard.

"I'll gladly fuck you," he all but growls out. "Then later, after we've recovered, you can return the favor."

His lips crash into mine, and he fumbles with the button of my jeans. The second they are undone, he pushes them down along with my boxers, freeing my erection.

"So fucking hot," he muses out loud as he grips my cock firmly, and my knees damn near buckle from the intense sensation.

He swipes the palm of his hand over my sensitive tip, collecting the precum to use as lube so he can stroke me without friction.

"Th-that feels too good," I stammer, trying not to blow my load instantly.

It's been a *long* time since I've been with anyone. And even though I jacked off last night, I'm already close to coming, like some young shit who just hit puberty.

Bennett lets go of me, and the lack of touch is welcome and missed at the same time.

"Ditch the rest of your clothes and get on the bed," he commands, stepping away to pull off his shirt.

"Who says you're in charge?" I question with a lifted brow.

Bennett smirks, shucking his pants and giving his *massive* cock a long, slow stroke. "Do you want me to fuck you or not?"

Without saying another word, I undress at lightning speed and climb onto the bed, earning me a chuckle at my eagerness that fills the quiet space.

I like a man who takes control in the bedroom just as much as I like to be in charge. Hopefully, when it's my turn to fuck Bennett, he'll be okay with me telling him what to do. So far, we are *very* compatible, and I love it.

"Lube and condoms are in the nightstand drawer," I inform him, waiting for him to join me on the bed. "But check the expiration date... it's been a while."

Turning my head, I watch my sexy man strut toward me with lust-filled eyes, looking like he's ready to eat me, and maybe he is.

"Those can wait," he says, crawling onto the bed like an animal on the prowl. He rubs my ass cheeks firmly with his large hands before pulling them apart, and a tingle of desperation shoots down my spine. "First, I want to get a taste of you."

The second the words are out of his lips, he leans down and licks me from my balls up.

"Jesus," I cry out, my head falling forward to rest on the blankets.

"Fucking delicious," he states, then dives in for another taste.

After a few laps, he stiffens his tongue, breaching my entrance and causing me to turn into a mewling mess. I've never been a loud lover, but something about the way that this sexy-as-fuck bodyguard is eating my ass has me losing all control. I pant, moan, and cry out as he sucks, licks, and kisses my pucker.

"Fuck... shit. More. God... yes. Please. Mm-hmm..."

Every time he fucks me with his tongue, I get louder, unable to form coherent sentences but not being able to keep quiet either. Bennett is as loud as I am as he hums his appreciation, and our combined lewd soundtrack turns me on even more.

"I love how vocal you are," Bennett states, coming up for air.

"I honestly never have been before. It's you. You do this to me," I barely get out, trying to catch my breath.

The fire that ignites behind his eyes tells me he likes knowing his effect on me is entirely different and new. It's primal and, dare I hope... possessive.

He moves to open the nightstand drawer, and my heart is racing as he checks the condom box, which must still be good because he grabs one and the bottle of lube.

"I see you've got a dildo in there. When did you use it last?" he asks. "I want to know how much prep you need because, after tasting that glorious hole, I'm even more desperate to be inside it."

His words have my cock bobbing between my legs, one hundred percent on board with him filling me as soon as possible. "It's been a few days, but I promise I don't need much prep. I like the burn, and I *need* you in me," I plead.

Bennett lets out a rumbly growl, and goose bumps cover my body. *Holy shit, that's hot.*

I assume he's going to get behind me again, so when he moves toward my head, his thick and long dick hanging right in front of my face, I'm caught a little off guard.

"I want you to suck me while I stretch you," he states, and precum drips from the tip of my swollen cock.

Sticking my tongue out, I take a long, slow lick of his mahogany cock, enjoying the way he groans. I swirl my tongue around the crown, and he leans over me, drizzling a dollop of lube onto my needy pucker. With the pad of his index finger, he swirls the liquid around before pushing and easily sliding inside me.

When I cry out, he shoves his hips forward, forcing his cock into my mouth. I gag a little, but my cock drips, loving the feeling of being used.

"You fucking like that, don't you?" he asks, twisting his finger inside me and thrusting into my mouth again.

I can't say words as my mouth is too full, so I nod around him and hum my positive response. I do my best to suck and swallow as he fucks my face and stretches me at the same time, but it's almost sensory overload, and I'm having a hard time keeping up. But with Bennett's moaning and the salty liquid of his precum coating my tongue, I don't think he minds that I'm not giving the best blow job I can right now.

After one more thrust down my throat, he pulls out, and I pant for air as he rolls me onto my back, dragging me to the end of the bed and standing between my legs. With lightning speed, he sheaths himself and pours an extra dollop of lube onto his erection. He uses one of his large hands to grip his cock firmly and the other to push my leg up so he's able to line himself up with my entrance.

"Are you ready, hot stuff?" he asks, the tip of his cock pressing firmly against my hole.

I nod so quickly it's almost funny. "Please fuck me," I beg.

Bennett's smirk is almost sinister, but I'm not scared.

He starts to enter me, and we both let out low groans of pleasure. His hands are now on my thighs, and he squeezes the muscles there as he fills me.

"You're so fucking tight," he grunts out.

"Ah-ah-ah" is the only thing I manage to choke out because actual words don't form.

It's been so long since I've been stretched like this or had another person inside me, and it's better than I remember. Maybe that's because of the person I'm with.

Once Bennett is seated all the way inside, he pauses and leans over me to steal a kiss. He's not hurried as he brushes his lips against mine, licking the seam, seeking entrance. I open for him, and our tongues dance as we make out.

He moves to trail kisses along my jaw, and when he reaches my ear, he pulls the lobe between his teeth.

"Do you have any idea how good you feel wrapped around my cock?" he questions, his breath hot on my face. "It's like you were made for me." After a long, slow lick up my neck, he lifts his upper body back and runs his hands up and down my thighs. "Ready for me to fuck you so good you'll never forget me?"

"I think you've already accomplished that," I murmur.

With a smirk, he says, "Nah, not yet I haven't, but I promise I'll succeed by the time we're done."

Tentatively, he pulls his hips back until he almost pops out before slamming into me hard.

"Yes," I yell.

"You like it hard, don't you?" he muses and repeats the motion.

I whimper. "Yes. Fuck me so hard. I want to feel it for days."

He hums in response, then lets go, plunging into me so hard it steals the breath from my lungs. The instant I can breathe again, I throw my head back and cry out with pleasure as he uses me.

"Fuck, you're so hot like this," he tells me. "Lying there mewling like a slut as I fuck you. But you're *my* slut, aren't you?"

"I-I'm yours."

Damn, I love his filthy words.

"That's right. You're mine, and I'm going to use this tight little fucking whore-hole of yours because it belongs to me now," he states. He won't find me arguing.

He continues to thrust into me hard and fast, and it feels so good my eyes roll into the back of my head. *How is he so goddamn good at fucking me?*

Spitting into the palm of his hand, he grabs my cock, stroking me in time with his movements. Each time he slides his hand up, he twists his wrist, and it's exactly what I need and rapidly brings me to the edge.

"I'm close," I moan out.

To my surprise, his hand slows and loosens, still stroking me, but not enough to get me off.

As I meet his eyes, the question in mine must be evident because he smirks at me and winks. "Not yet. I'm not letting you come so soon. You're mine now, and I'm claiming this little hole thoroughly before either of us is getting off. I'm not going to draw this out too long, though. Not right now. You're not ready for that yet.

"But one day soon, I will keep pounding you and stay buried inside you for hours on end, without stopping. I'll use my thick cock to massage your prostate and milk you nearly dry before letting you come. I want to fuck you till you're exhausted and limp in my arms, begging me to let you come. Then, and only then, will we both detonate."

Fuck, this man is hot. His words make me mewl as they drive right into my brain and cement themselves. I want what he promised more than anything. Part of me now craves to give in to him completely. To submit and give myself over to his will. It's a feeling I've never had before, and it's almost shocking how much I want it.

It's like Bennett is reading my mind when he whispers, "Mm... yes. I can see how much you want that too, how much it excites you. Fuck, seeing how much you want it makes my balls ache and has them rising so I can spill inside of you right now.

"Just think, though, as much as I plan on claiming and taking you, I plan on giving to you in return. I want you to take me the same way. Fuck me, drill me, pound me, push me, and hold me down with your weight as you drive into me relentlessly. Take me however you want and claim me right back."

Bennett's words are like fuel added to an already raging inferno, drawing us both so close to an explosion of epic proportions.

A layer of sweat covers our bodies, and Bennett's dark brows pinch together as he grunts with each thrust. Our skin smacks together loudly and is mixed with our pants and cries of pleasure as we grow ever closer to the apex.

He tightens his hand on my cock again, instantly driving me wild and forcing me to desperately fist the sheets as I try to hold out.

"Come for me," Bennett commands, the fingers of his other hand digging punishingly into my upper thigh as he chases his orgasm.

It only takes two more thrusts and tugs, and I'm exploding, covering my stomach and chest in cum. A drop even hits my chin, and I'm not sure I've ever released such a big load in my life.

"Jesus. Fucking. Christ," my man yells as my channel squeezes around him.

He comes with a roar, his body shaking with the intensity of his orgasm, and it gives me this heady sensation of pride.

"Holy shit," he murmurs as he falls forward, catching himself on his forearms so as not to crush me. "I'm not sure I've ever come that hard."

I chuckle and rub his back. "I feel the exact same way."

He smiles, then his eyes zero in on my chin, and he licks the drop of cum away. "Fuck, you're tasty," he whispers before kissing me.

He slips his tongue into my mouth, and I taste myself, which is sexy as sin, and if my cock wasn't so spent, I'm sure it would be coming to life again.

"Want to have a shower and then a nap?" I ask.

He gives me a quizzical look. "You're tired?"

"A little, but I mainly need the rest so that I have the energy to fuck you later."

His eyes light up at the words, and he moves to pull out of me. I'm definitely sore and will be feeling that way for some time, but that's exactly what I wanted.

Bennett offers me his hand, and I take it, using his support to stand, but instead of pulling me to the bathroom, he envelops me in a hug.

We hold each other for a while, and I love the simplicity of this intimate moment. It's special.

Whatever happens between Bennett and me, I won't be forgetting this.

Chapter Fifteen

BENNETT

Soft music plays from the speakers as Archer and I sit in the studio, waiting for Aria and the rest of the band members to show up. We're holding hands, and my man seems calm as a cucumber.

Can he sense how nervous I am right now?

We spoke with Aria early this morning after some lovely wake-up blow jobs and told her about our relationship. She was over-the-moon excited but told us we needed to tell the band. Since we are going on tour in less than two weeks, it's important they are filled in now. Neither Archer nor I want to keep our relationship a secret, but usually, most people wait more than one day to tell all of their friends they are seeing someone. Unfortunately, we don't have the luxury of waiting because we all will be together in close quarters soon.

Thankfully, a rehearsal was already planned for today, so we didn't have to call everyone over for an out-of-the-blue meeting. That would have been much more awkward.

Aria let the band's PR team know about the relationship in case anything got leaked, and Archer signed the paperwork Nixon sent over. We also informed him that we were now officially in a relationship.

With all those important people aware, it's time to talk to the band. Archer keeps assuring me everything will be fine, and I hope he's right.

I'm not sure he'll stay with me if we don't have the blessing of his friends.

"How is my annoying brother and the man dating him today?" Aria asks, strutting into the studio with a mischievous gleam in her eyes.

"How am I annoying?" Archer questions, his brows pulled together in confusion.

"The fact that you exist isn't enough reason?" she teases.

Archer rolls his eyes. "I've heard some twins eat the other one in utero. I should have done that. It would have made my life so much easier."

"Pshaw," she disagrees. "Your life would be empty without me. I am sunshine and rainbows compacted into a cute and petite package. Plus, you would be utterly lost without me. You'd have no idea where you were going or what you were doing."

"I could hire someone else," he counters, making his twin gasp.

"Don't say words like that. You'll make me think you don't love me anymore," she replies in mock horror with a hand placed on her chest like his words actually wounded her.

"You know I love you, even if you do drive me crazy," Archer grumbles.

Aria skips over to us and places a wet kiss on her brother's cheek. "I love you too, you weirdo."

He sighs, wiping his cheek, but the smirk he's trying to hide peaks through.

"When are you going to tell the fam jam about your new boyfriend?" Aria asks.

He shrugs. "I'm not sure. Isn't it too soon to tell the family? We literally started dating yesterday. I'm pretty sure I wouldn't have told anyone this early if it wasn't for the nature of my job. Relationships deserve time to breathe before others are brought in."

I agree wholeheartedly with Archer, but I understand why we have to do it this way. Although the idea of telling my parents isn't a nauseating one. It feels right, which I know is weird since we've only known each other for less than a week.

"Whenever you're ready, I'm cool with telling your family," I assure Archer in case he's worried I don't want anyone else to know.

My sexy country musician turns to me and smiles warmly. "Thanks, I'll think about it."

I kiss his cheek, and the door to the studio opens.

"The life of the party has arrived," Landon shouts as he walks in and plops onto a couch.

"More like the pain in my ass," Aria murmurs.

"What did I do this time?" he whines, sounding like a child.

"I'm not sure yet, but I'll figure it out soon enough," she responds, sticking her tongue out at him.

"Is there something going on between them?" I whisper to Archer, who lifts his shoulders with an *I have no clue* look.

Brando arrives next followed by Joseph, who is only a few minutes behind.

"Sorry I'm late," Joseph says, looking a little disheveled. "Shit kind of hit the fan between Amy and me last night. I slept in my car, so sorry if I stink."

"Why didn't you call one of us?" Brando asks.

"I didn't want to be a bother. But I am in need of a couch to crash on for a couple of nights if someone doesn't mind. Even though we're fighting, it doesn't feel right to kick Amy to the curb. I told her she has a week to get everything sorted out and her shit gone. I was thinking about giving her longer, but I'm scared she'll change the locks while we are gone on tour, and I don't need that headache."

"I told you she had crazy eyes," Landon mutters.

Aria smacks him upside the head. "Be nice," she scolds him.

"You can stay at my place as long as you need," Brando offers. "And no need to sleep on the couch. I've got plenty of spare bedrooms."

Joseph smiles at his friend. "Thanks, man, I appreciate it."

"Before we get rehearsal started, I wanted to say something," Archer announces once everything is sorted out between Joseph and Brando. "Things are *very* new, but since we'll all be on tour together, I wanted you to be aware that Bennett and I are dating."

Nobody says anything at first, and the silence is almost deafening. When looks are shared between the band members, my stomach rolls.

What is going on?

Brando finally smiles after a few seconds pass, which would probably ease my worries if it wasn't for how grumpy Joseph and Landon appear. The two men stand, and I'm not sure what is about to happen, but my guard is up. They reach for their wallets instead of walking toward Archer and me, leaving me even more confused.

What the hell is going on?

They hand Brando a hundred-dollar bill each, and Archer gasps. "Did you bet on us?" he shouts.

Brando laughs. "Yep, but in a good way. When we met Bennett the other day, we saw something between you two, so we bet on when you would get together. My bet was within the week, so these assholes have to pay up."

"I thought it would be while we were on tour," Joseph admits.

"I figured it would be at least a couple of months," Landon tells us.

"You're not upset?" I question, and they all shake their heads.

"Nah, you seem like a cool guy. But if you hurt him, we *will* have to kill you," Brando says, and the rest of the guys nod in solidarity.

"I'd expect nothing less, but I wouldn't be able to live with myself if I hurt Archer," I reply, looking at my man as I speak. "He's too special."

He blushes at my words and playfully shoves my shoulder. "Okay, with that out of the way, let's rehearse."

I sit back with a smile and take in the free concert.

Refusing to let my fears hold me back anymore, I find myself, dare I say, happy.

It can only get better from here, right?

Chapter Sixteen

ARCHER

Bennett and I are curled up on my couch, half asleep, when a random thought pops into my head. "What do you think about getting tested?" I ask.

Bennett moves me so we are face to face, staring intently into my eyes. "You want to go bare?" he questions, and my face heats as I dip my chin.

I'm not sure why I'm embarrassed all of a sudden. It's not like we haven't fucked already, but this is a whole different step, and we only recently started our relationship.

"I know it's fast, but I don't want barriers between us. I'll be honest. I've been bare with one partner in the past, but it's been a long time, and I want to experience that connection with you. But of course, only if you want that too," I add on quickly so he hopefully doesn't feel pressured. "If you do want that, I would love for us to get tested together. I'm already on PrEP, but I also want to prove to you that I'm negative."

Bennett presses his lips to mine for a slow, passionate kiss. When we break for air, there is a content smile on his lips. "I trust you, but I'd love to get tested. I'm also on PrEP, but I've never been bare with anyone."

"We can wait if you aren't ready. This is a big step, and we only made things official yesterday."

Bennett shakes his head and kisses my nose, which is entirely too sweet, but I love it. "I want this with you," he assures me. "Yes, it's fast, but it feels right."

I love that we are on the same page, and I don't want to wait, so I pull out my phone and find us a clinic to get tested today. "We've got one hour to get ready. "Want to shower with me?" I ask, waggling my brows suggestively.

"I'll grab the condoms and meet you in the bathroom," he replies.

A shiver of anticipation flows through my body, and I race to the bathroom, the deep timbre of Bennett's laughter echoing behind me.

Our shower takes a lot longer than it would if we were showering alone, but this is much more fun.

When we finally get out, we head to the clinic.

This excited energy runs over my skin while my blood is being taken. I'm over the moon to take this next step with this man.

"Please tell me you're not leaving tonight," I plead when we return to my house.

We were promised to have our results within twenty-four hours, and even though I'm confident we will both have completely negative results, I still can't wait to present them to Bennett.

"If you want me here, there is nowhere else I'd rather be," he assures me, pulling me into his arms for a sweet embrace.

I rest my head against his chest, my lips turned up, and this feeling of contentment washes over me. "I want you here."

He holds me silently, and I listen to the beating of his heart. How is it that I feel so at ease with him so quickly? But I refuse to second-guess things. Yes, it's fast, but why must there be a specific timeline for things to feel right? Some people are together for years, and they break up, so time really means nothing.

"Want to cuddle in bed?" I question, my eyelids growing heavy.

"Absolutely," he replies, letting me go but grabbing my hand as we make our way to my bedroom.

I already don't want to let him go, which should be scary but feels right.

OVER THE NEXT FEW days, we spend as much time together as possible. We probably would have even if we weren't in a relationship, but it's different now that he's more than my bodyguard.

He holds my hand when I meet with my band and shares secret looks with me as I go for costume fittings. Every night, we fall asleep in each other's arms, except for one, and I missed him like crazy that night.

We've fallen into an easy routine, and I can't see my life without Bennett, which is insane. We've only been together a week now, but nothing has ever felt more right, and I refuse to overthink it. I'm loving getting to know my boyfriend and growing this new relationship.

Tonight, we are having dinner with my family, and it's obvious he's nervous.

"Are you sure they are going to be cool with this?" he asks me for the hundredth time as he parks in front of their house.

"They already love you. I promise they are going to be fine with our relationship," I assure him.

"Whose vehicle is that?" he questions, pointing to a car in front of us that I've never seen.

There haven't been any new letters from my supposed stalker, and no one has been seen on my property, so I have taken it as a positive.

But now, with Bennett on edge and an unknown vehicle at my parents' house, I'm a little anxious.

"I don't know. Maybe someone is visiting a neighbor," I point out, hopeful, but Bennett doesn't take his eyes off the car.

"Don't move," he tells me firmly as he grabs his phone and calls Aria on speaker.

"Why are you two sitting in the car and not coming inside?" she asks when she answers the phone.

I look at the big front windows of my parents' house, and I spot her spying on us.

"Do you recognize the vehicle parked in front of us?" Bennett checks with her.

She giggles. "Yes, but it's a surprise, so hurry up and get in here."

The line goes quiet, and Bennett shakes his head. "I don't love surprises," he grumbles.

I reach over to grab his hand. "Come on," I encourage him. "I'm sure it's nothing crazy, and now you know the car isn't anything to be worried about."

He gets out of the vehicle and walks with me up the stone path, his hand in mine, and this moment is fucking perfect.

How is it that within less than two weeks of knowing someone, a person can already picture spending forever with them? That's how I feel about Bennett.

"This is an interesting development," Dad says when we walk through the door, still holding hands.

"Is that good or bad?" Bennett whispers to me.

"So far, good, but time will tell," Dad replies. "Chantel," he yells into the kitchen. "Archer brought a boyfriend with him."

The quick clicking of crutches alerts us that my mom is on her way. "He has a boyfriend?" she calls out, and when she finally gets to us, she gasps, but a smile slowly spreads across her face. "Oh, this makes me happy. Come on in. We have someone for you to meet."

My brows pull together because I have no idea what she's talking about.

Who is here?

Is that what the surprise is?

We follow my parents into the kitchen, where *all* my siblings are visiting. I gasp when my eyes land on my baby sister, and I rush to her, pulling her into my arms.

"What the hell are you doing here?" I ask Stefanie, squeezing her tightly.

"My costar broke his leg. The crew needs to figure out how to pivot, so we all got a week off. Figured I'd come back and visit the family," she says. "What's this I hear about a boyfriend?"

I take a step back, grabbing Bennett's hand and smiling wide. "Stefanie, this is Bennett, my bodyguard and boyfriend. Bennett, this is my younger sister, Stefanie."

"Bodyguard *and* boyfriend?" she questions, but she winks before Bennett can think she's serious. "Nice."

"It's nice to meet you," Bennett says, reaching his hand out to her, but she slaps it away.

"We're huggers in this family," she tells him, pulling him in for a hug. "I might be the youngest girl in this family, but if you hurt my big brother, I will cut your dick off, shove it down your throat, and laugh as I watch you die." Her words are quiet but loud enough for me to hear. "Now, who's ready to eat? Mom made lasagna," she announces with a giant grin when she steps back.

"Your sister is kind of scary," Bennett whispers to me.

"Totally, but in the best way," I reply, and he chuckles.

"I love when people are protective over those who deserve it," he states, and that's my family to a *T*. We stand up for each other and would never let someone get away with hurting one of our own.

We all sit down at the table and pass the food around, chatting lively as Stefanie fills us in on all the gossip from the show she's been working on.

"Mind if I steal your boyfriend for a minute?" Dad asks once we've finished eating.

"Stefanie already gave him the *if you hurt him, I'll kill you* speech," I inform him, and he laughs.

"I figured as much, but I'd like to talk to Bennett alone if that's okay."

I look to my sexy bodyguard, and he shrugs. "I'll be fine. I don't mind talking with your dad." He kisses my temple and stands to follow Dad outside to the back porch.

I'm dying to know what they are going to talk about, but I respect them both too much to eavesdrop. Instead, I hang out with my siblings in the living room, catching up.

My dad and Bennett spend a long while talking, and when they finally come back inside, I'm dying to grill him on what my dad had to say, but now isn't the time for that. It will have to wait for the drive home.

Bennett sits next to me and puts his arm around my shoulder in a comfortable and relaxed manner, and almost instinctively, I lean into him, loving that we can be like this in front of my family. It's amazing how at ease he is, and that makes me beyond happy. My family is my life, and I don't know what I would do if things were awkward between them and my new boyfriend. Thankfully, I don't have to find out.

After several hours of visiting, it's time for us to leave.

"Don't be a stranger," Mom says, hugging Bennett and me. "Either of you," she adds, staring directly at Bennett with those words.

"We won't," I assure her before embracing my siblings. "Am I going to see you again before my tour?" I ask Stefanie.

"I'll make sure we do," she promises and gives me a sloppy kiss on my cheek before whispering in my ear. "I really like how happy you seem right now."

I wave her off and roll my eyes, but she isn't wrong. Bennett has brought a new sort of joy into my life, something I never want to lose.

The goodbyes drag on, but eventually, Bennett and I escape.

"My dad didn't scare you off, did he?" I ask when we're in the comfort of his SUV.

Bennett chuckles and shakes his head. "Not at all," he assures me. "Almost the opposite."

I quirk a brow. "Care to elaborate?"

"Nope," he says with that perfect smile I'm growing to love plastered on his lips. "Not today."

I pout, which only results in a boisterous laugh from the man quickly taking up a permanent space in my heart.

"Didn't think it was possible for a man your size to look so cute, but here you are looking adorable with that pout," he teases, and I roll my eyes, which has Bennett laughing harder.

"Your dad is a good man, and I love how protective he is of your family. Let's just leave it at that for now, okay?"

I nod, reaching over the console to hold his hand while he drives me home.

"Are you staying the night?" I ask as he parks in front of my door.

There has only been one night this week that Bennett hasn't stayed, and I missed his warm body against mine.

"I could be persuaded to stay," he replies with almost a purr.

The corners of my lips turn up, and I run my fingers over his shoulder. "What's a boy gotta do to make his sexy bodyguard stay?"

"Breed me," he offers, but it's more like a plea.

My hand freezes on his shoulder, and my cock goes hard.

Our test results came back the day after we got tested, but we've still been using condoms. I think we were both nervous to bring up the conversation. It's a huge step to go bare with a partner, and we've only been together a week, but the time doesn't really matter to me. I have more trust in Bennett than I did in my last boyfriend, who I was with for over a year. The saying *when you know, you know* rings true here. I *know* I want to lose the condoms and feel *all* of Bennett.

"Are you sure?" I ask, needing to clarify. This isn't something I want to assume.

He nods, leaning over to kiss me. His full lips are soft and controlling as the kiss turns from gentle to all-consuming in the blink of an eye. I moan into his mouth, and his tongue dives in, dancing with mine as we make out in the car. Heavy panting, wet smacking of lips, and needy mewls fill the small space and have my cock leaking in my underwear, desperate for more.

"Need... you... inside... now," I say between kisses since Bennett won't let up for me to get more than one word out at a time, which I secretly love.

With a nip to my lip, Bennett finally backs up, staring at me with lust-filled eyes.

"You look so hot with kiss-swollen lips," he tells me, running the pad of his thumb over my bottom lip.

He grinds his teeth, growling as he opens the car door like it's taking all of his strength not to kiss me again. "Let's go so you can fuck me."

My cock pushes painfully against the confines of my clothes, and I race to get out of the car and into my house as fast as possible. Neither of us wants to wait for the bedroom, so the instant the door is shut behind us, our mouths crash together, and I push Bennett up against the wall.

One thing I've really enjoyed about being with this man is that he could so easily overpower me, and at times, he does, but he also lets me take control when I want it. I also love it when he doesn't easily give in, and we fight for power. It's so fucking hot.

As we kiss, we frantically strip out of our clothes, desperate to be skin to skin.

"I love how much you leak," Bennett notes once I'm naked, grabbing my cock and smearing the precum around as he strokes me.

My head falls back, and a deep moan slips past my lips. "Imagine how good it's going to feel inside you without any barriers," I tell him, and he licks his lips like the thought alone is making him hungry for it.

"Can't wait."

"Couch, now," I demand, grabbing his hand to lead him to the side table, where a bottle of lube is so we don't have to climb the stairs to my bedroom. "Kneel," I instruct, gesturing to the couch, and he obeys instantly.

Bennett's knees are on the loveseat's cushions, and his arms are on the back. It has his ass sticking out in the most ideal position.

I run a hand up his perfectly toned back, loving how his muscles twitch and noticing how his warm brown skin contrasts with my paleness.

"You're so hot," I tell him, squirting lube onto my fingers. I warm it up before pressing a finger to his pucker and circling it. Then, leaning over his body as I tease his hole, I lick his ear, and he turns his face for me so I can steal a kiss.

Our tongues move together, and I push my finger inside him, loving the needy moan that escapes his lips.

"Sooo f-fucking goood," he cries out, and I twist the digit in him, searching for his pleasure spot. And when he shouts, his back bowing, I'm certain I found it and use that moment to slide in a second finger.

"Your fingers feel sooo good," he moans out. "But I want your cock."

I snicker. "Maybe I want to make you come like this?" I tease, pushing against his prostate again, massaging it this time.

Bennett pants, his cock twitching between his legs.

"P-please," he begs, and this warm feeling of pride takes over my body.

The big, strong bodyguard who oozes control and command is begging for my cock right now. It's a heady feeling I cherish.

"Please, what?" I ask, gently pushing in a third finger.

"Fuuuck," he breathes out.

The smirk on my face never leaves as I stretch his needy hole.

"Pl-please get inside me. I... I need your cock in me. I w-want you to fill me with your cum." His pleading has my cock leaking even more, and there is no way I can hold off any longer.

"Since you asked so nicely," I reply, tenderly sliding my fingers out.

Bennett lets out a little whimper, and I can't help but chuckle. "Don't worry, baby, you won't be empty for long," I assure him, pouring more lube onto my cock and lining up behind him. "Ready?"

He nods rapidly, his head almost bouncing off the couch.

I snicker a little, but it morphs into a groan when I push my hips forward and start to enter him. His channel is so fucking tight it's choking my cock and causing my eyes to roll into the back of my head. Taking a deep breath and blowing it out slowly, I try to stop myself from blowing my load prematurely. How is it that removing the thinnest barrier makes all the difference? I can feel *everything*. It's almost too much.

With steady pressure, I keep pushing forward until my balls are pressed firmly against his body, then I pause. Bennett is panting heavily, resting his head against the couch, his back rising and falling with his breaths.

"Are you okay?" I check.

"You... feel... so... good," he tells me between breaths.

I smile, leaning down to kiss him. "So do you, hot stuff," I whisper against his lips.

Kissing him like a starved man, I give us both time to adjust.

"I need you to fuck me now," he pleads when I nibble along his jaw and pull his earlobe between my teeth.

I grin, licking the lobe before straightening and gripping his hips firmly.

"With fucking pleasure." I pull my hips away, then slam forward, driving into him hard.

Bennett cries out in bliss, his head falling back. I take that opportunity to wrap my hand around his throat, pulling him to me again so his back is resting against my chest.

"You were made for me, weren't you?" I growl into his ear, snapping my hips forward and backward at a rapid speed.

"Y-yes."

I turn his face toward mine and devour his lips, fucking him with all I've got. His moans and cries are swallowed down and muffled by my kiss, leaving only the smacking of our skin coming together to fill the room. A thin layer of sweat covers our bodies, and I'm almost positive Bennett can feel the rapid beating of my heart against his back.

"Spit," I command, letting go of his throat and holding my palm up to his mouth.

He does as he's told, and I lower my hand to his perfect dick. With my other hand, I press in between his shoulder blades, and he braces himself on the couch again.

While I jack him off, I lift one of my feet to rest beside his knees, giving me a better angle, and when he cries out, I know I've found his prostate again. Holding that position, I nail his prostate over and over again and stroke his cock in rhythm with my thrusts.

"Are you close?" I ask as my balls draw up, and a tingling sensation covers my entire body, letting me know it won't be long before I'm filling him up.

"S-sooo close," he tells me, and I pick up the speed of my hand.

After a few more strokes, warm liquid covers my fist and shoots onto my leather couch, and Bennett shouts, "Fuuuck."

He comes, and his channel clamps around me, sending me over the edge with him. My orgasm is so intense it steals my breath and pulls a deep, guttural growl from me as I fill him with my cum.

Once I've emptied my balls, I lean over him and hold him until my breathing has evened.

"That was amazing," I whisper when I can speak again, and Bennett nods with a sex- drunk look on his face.

I gently slide out of him, watching in awe as my cum drips from his hole. "So hot," I murmur, using my thumb to push it back in and smirk as he shivers from being oversensitive.

"It feels so slippery and messy," Bennett notes as more of my cum slides down his legs.

"You like it, though, right?" I check.

"Oh yes. I can't wait until I get to fill you."

A shiver of anticipation runs down my spine. It's been a long time since I've experienced that, but I bet it will be even better with Bennett.

"Do you want a shower before we go to sleep?" I ask.

"Yes. I need to wash the cum out of my ass."

I kiss his cheek and say, "Why don't you run up and get started? I want to wipe down the couch quickly. I think dried cum is going to be harder to clean."

"Good thinking. Also, thank God for leather couches," Bennett says, carefully walking away with funny steps as he clenches his ass cheeks.

I can't help but laugh at the sight, but there is also this heady feeling that *I'm* the reason he's walking like that. It's *my* load in his ass that he's trying to keep in and fuck, that's hot. Now I'm dying to know what it will feel like to be filled with Bennett's load.

Chapter Seventeen

BENNETT

THE PARKING LOT IS empty except for the line of buses and a few random vehicles, and I'm on high alert. Some belong to the paparazzi, while others are just passing through to drop people off. I was warned that at least a few paparazzi would be here today, but the sight of them has my skin crawling.

I understand they have a job to do, but almost none respect boundaries, which bothers me.

"Ready for your first tour?" Archer asks, and I nod.

I still can't believe how fast the past few weeks have flown by.

My sexy country music star's face is lit up with pure joy and excitement. It eases my nerves a little. The way his full lips are turned upright has me desperate to kiss him, but I have to refrain for now. If I pulled him into me, someone would certainly snap a picture, and I'm not ready to be under a microscope yet. That will come eventually, but I like that only those closest to us know about our relationship.

My parents were ecstatic when I called them, and my mom was immediately fishing to see how serious we were about each other. I wouldn't be surprised if she starts asking about grandchildren in the near future.

Two weeks isn't a long time to be with someone, but somehow, it's enough time for me to know I don't *ever* want to let Archer go. He makes my days brighter and fills them with laughter and light, not to mention the unbelievable sex.

"As ready as I'll ever be," I reply dryly, hating how grumpy the words come across because it causes Archer's smile to drop. I quickly add, "Don't lose that smile. I'm just anxious about this whole thing."

He visibly relaxes a little. "I understand you're looking out for me, but we haven't heard anything from the creepy stalker since the last tour ended. Let's take no news as good news," he pleads, and I sigh with a short nod.

I don't hold the same sentiments, but there's no use in arguing. I just have to be on my A-game while we are away from home. This whole tour would have been canceled if I had it my way. Traveling from city to city adds a bunch of variables I don't like, but I trust my team and know we can keep Archer and the rest of his band as safe as humanly possible. I'm pretty sure most of my apprehension right now is my feelings for Archer. Who wouldn't want to keep their boyfriend safe?

I'm confident we'll do our best, but shit happens. That's what worries me the most.

"Who's ready to rock?" Landon yells as he struts over to us.

"It's too early for you to be so loud," Aria grumbles from where she is leaning against the bus, going over some notes on her tablet.

"Don't try to dampen my excitement," he argues.

Aria pinches the bridge of her nose and walks over to us. "I know you're a bodyguard, but is there any chance you're a hired hitman on the side because I could use that kind of service right about now," she whispers, making sure it's loud enough for Landon to hear.

"I'm sorry, I don't, but I might know a guy," I tell her with a shrug and a wink.

"And here I thought we were gonna be friends," Landon whines.

"Didn't anyone ever teach you not to bite the hand that feeds you?" I ask him. "I'm completely aware that Aria is the one who runs things around here. There is no way I want to get on her bad side."

Landon pouts, and Aria kisses my cheek. "I knew I liked you," she says into my ear but is holding eye contact with Landon. "Smart guys are hot."

Archer's brows are lifted when I glance his way, and he's giving me a *what the fuck is happening* stare.

I twist my lips, silently replying *I have no idea* because I really don't. If I were to take a wild guess, I'd say Landon and Aria are hiding something, like a secret relationship. I could be completely off base, but I make a mental note to ask Archer if they've always been like this because the animosity between the two of them is coming across like a bad act.

Thankfully, the rest of the conversations aren't too awkward as we wait for Joseph and Brandon. Once they arrive, everyone gets settled on the bus, and I excuse myself to brief my team after giving Archer a quick peck on the lips that has his face lighting up with desire.

I'm seriously beginning to second-guess my decision about keeping things under wraps because I want him to see that look all the time. Maybe it would be best to come out with it now because keeping my hands to myself in public isn't as easy as I thought it would be.

"Hey, boss man," Rip greets when I exit the bus.

"Everyone ready for a quick recap of what is expected today?" I check with my team, and they all nod. "Rip, you will be on the main bus with me. Henley and Michael, you will be on the first crew bus, and Carter and Cole, you will be on the second crew bus."

The team is already aware of this information, but I always like to give reminders. It keeps communication open and minds clear.

"Whenever stops are made, one of you must get off first to confirm it is safe, and the other will bring up the rear. Earpieces are to be worn at all times when we are not on the buses, and your phones are not to be shut off for any reason. If I need to get a hold of you, you better be available. Other than that, today is an easy day of traveling. Remember, I'm always available for a call or text if you think there is information I need to know about."

Everyone nods in response, and I smile. "Thanks for being a part of this. You are all amazing men, and I'm positive you will do your best to ensure this tour runs smoothly without any hiccups."

With those parting words, most my team walks away to climb onto their assigned buses, and Rip follows me for a final walk around.

Once I'm confident nothing looks out of order, we enter the bus where the band waits.

"Are we good to go?" Leo, the lead bus driver, asks after I close the door.

"Everything looks good on my end," I confirm.

He smiles and grabs his walkie-talkie to let the rest of the drivers know it's time to head out.

"This is a snazzy bus," Rip notes, looking around at the posh interior of an extremely expensive tour bus.

"Welcome to the life of the rich and the famous," Aria teases. "You were already shown which bunk is yours, right?"

"Yes, ma'am, Bennett showed me when I arrived this morning."

Aria places her hand on her chest and fakes a gasp. "I am nowhere near old enough to be a *ma'am*. Please do me a favor and *never* call me that again."

Rip chuckles nervously, grabbing the back of his neck, and his cheeks are turning a light shade of red. I'm not sure if he's concerned that he actually offended Aria or if it's an attraction thing. "Sorry, would you like me just to call you Aria?"

"Yes, please," she says with a megawatt grin, giving his cheek a quick peck of appreciation. "Now, come meet the rest of the crew."

Rip follows her like a lost puppy, and I can't help but think this could be a disaster. I'll keep my fingers crossed that this doesn't turn into some sort of awkward love triangle between Rip, Aria, and Landon. If worse comes to worse, I can get another member of our team to switch places with him, but hopefully, it won't come to that. I like working closely with Rip. My entire team is amazing, and I trust them all with my life, but there is something about how Rip and I work together that makes him an easy choice as my second-in-command.

Aria introduces Rip to everyone, and I sit next to Archer, who beams at me and gives me a quick kiss before getting comfortable for the drive ahead.

Archer holds my hand as everyone talks, and it's crazy how at ease we are right now. You'd think it would be awkward now that we are out of our little bubble, but everyone on this bus knows about and supports us, so it's like an extension of that bubble.

Once we go public, I'm sure it will be a different story.

Thankfully, peaceful moments like this ease some of the stress I'm under and will continue to be until we figure out who the stalker is and get him arrested.

Chapter Eighteen

ARCHER

The stadium is bustling with workers setting up the stage and making sure everything is perfect for our concert tonight. I love the busy environment almost as much as I love the energy the crowd gives off.

Touring takes a lot out of a person, but there is almost a high you receive when you hear your fans screaming all the words to every song. It's what I live for. Writing and recording are cathartic and what pays most of the bills but performing is what fills my soul.

"Why is there a shrimp platter on the buffet table?" Aria asks a lady with a venomous tone.

"Oh shit," I whisper to Bennett, who lifts a brow at me, obviously wondering what's going on. "Landon has a severe shellfish allergy, and Aria is very diligent about noting that anytime we hire a caterer."

Bennett's eyes go wide. "If they didn't listen to the instructions, there is a possibility of cross-contamination."

I nod, my stomach rolling at the possibility of one of my band members getting seriously sick because of an oversight like this.

"I'm sorry. I'm just the delivery person," the lady says, her voice shaking.

"Take it all back," Aria demands. "I'll call Marla and inform her that she won't be getting paid the remainder of the contracted amount, and we'll also be requesting our deposit back. This is unacceptable. One of the band members could have been sent to the hospital over this."

The lady nods and rushes to pack up the food.

"What are you going to do?" I ask, walking toward my sister.

"Call every pizza joint in town and see what they can do," she says with defeat.

I place my hand on her shoulder and give it a squeeze. "You've got this," I reassure her.

She offers me a small smile. "I know, it's always disappointing when things like this happen. Can you let the band know supper will be late?"

"I've got you covered," I reply and head to the dressing rooms.

"Is supper ready?" Brando asks when I step into the shared space area.

I shake my head. "Sorry, there was an issue with the caterer. They had a shrimp platter on the table." Brando gasps, completely aware of how bad that is. "So now Aria has to find a last-minute replacement."

"Shit," Brando replies. "At least I've got a bag of chips to tide me over for now."

"Aria always comes through, but this is gonna put things behind a little."

"What's behind?" Landon questions as he enters the room with Joseph and Rip behind him.

"Supper. The caterer fucked up and somehow missed the note about your allergy," I tell him.

Landon growls and balls his fists at his side. "Seriously? Who the fuck does that? I know exactly how Aria words her emails, and it's impossible to miss."

I get why he's pissed. An incident last year sent him to the hospital and had him missing two shows. Thankfully, the bass player of the opening band was able to fill in for us, but it wasn't ideal.

"I'll be more diligent going forward," Aria assures everyone, appearing in the doorway.

"This wasn't your fault," I remind her.

She sighs. "I know it wasn't my fault, but it still happened. So, from now on, I'm going to do more research on the caterers we use. I'm going to make sure nothing like this ever happens again. I'm sorry."

Landon shakes his head, grabbing her hand. "Don't blame yourself. Clearly, you caught the mistake before I got sick, and I'm assuming you already have more food on the way."

Aria's cheeks turn a light shade of pink, and she nods, not pulling her hand away from Landon's, which is interesting.

"More food is on its way. I was able to find a restaurant not far from here that doesn't have any shellfish on site. They promised an amazing platter, so fingers crossed that the food is decent. It should be here in about an hour and a half."

"See? You've got us covered, so stop beating yourself up."

When Landon drops my sister's hand, he continues to stare at her with a look of adoration. If they think they are fooling anyone with their fake fighting, they've got another thing coming.

It's obvious they are trying to hide their feelings for each other but are doing a piss-poor job of it. I'll have to bug her about it when we are alone.

"Is the audio team ready for us to do a sound check now?" I ask Aria, wanting to fill the time with something productive.

"I'll check and get back to you soon," she replies, rushing out of the room.

"What's going on with you and Aria?" Brando asks the question I'm sure the majority of us are thinking.

"Nothing," he scoffs, but none of us are buying it. "She's like an annoying sister, but I didn't want her feeling bad about this."

"Suuure," Joseph says with a smirk.

Landon rolls his eyes. "Believe what you want, but nothing is going on between Aria and me."

"And the sky is green," Bennett adds, which has everyone but Landon busting a gut.

Landon flips us the bird and grumbles something under his breath about us being a bunch of assholes.

"The audio team is ready for you," Aria announces, sticking her head into the room.

"Come on, let's go make sure we sound amazing," I call out and follow Aria to the stage with Bennett at my side and Rip following behind the rest of the band.

I thought it would be awkward as hell having this much security, but it's oddly comforting. Maybe that's because I love having Bennett with me at all times, or it's because I'm extremely confident that he won't let anyone hurt me. I'm still not as anxious as everyone else about my stalker problem, but if they do try to get to me, they won't get far.

Arriving at the stage, I smile at the roadie who hands me my guitar and walk out to where a microphone is waiting. I make sure my in-ear monitors are in properly and wait for the cue to start.

Even though there isn't a crowd yet, I'm already getting the adrenaline rush of performing, and I allow myself to get lost in the song.

Once everything is confirmed to be working as it should, we head back to our shared space and wait for the food to arrive.

The only thing that could make this day better would be the ability to hold hands with Bennet in public. I hate that I'm having to spend hours not touching him because I'm craving it more than I thought I would. At least in private, we get to be together, which matters most to me.

I never would have guessed I would become the clingy boyfriend type. I want to ask Bennett if he feels the same way, but I don't want to pressure him into something he's not ready for. We said we would wait to make our relationship public, and I want to respect his wishes. But if it so happens that Bennett is willing to throw caution to the wind, nothing would make me happier than to shout about our relationship from the rooftops.

Chapter Nineteen

BENNETT

So far, tonight has gone perfectly, besides the shellfish incident, but my hackles are up as the meet and greet draws closer. Obviously, this event has been planned with my team for some time now, but that doesn't make me less anxious.

Before the main event starts, the band is meeting with Brando's cousin, Chase, to sign a few things for a charity auction his university is putting on. At least that gives me time to breathe before I'll be on extra high alert.

"Look at you, growing up way too fast," Brando says to his cousin as he walks into the main lounge area.

The two men hug each other, then Brando turns toward me. "This is my little cousin, Chase," he introduces.

"Nice to meet you. The Koala's killed it last year," I say, mentioning his college football team. "You're quite the quarterback. Do you plan on going pro once you're eligible?"

His smile is bright, lighting up his face. "I hope so. Football is all I've ever known, and I'm not that smart, so if I don't get drafted, I'm not sure what I'll do."

Brando gives his cousin a gentle shove. "Don't talk about yourself like that," he scolds.

Chase shrugs. "I don't think of it as a negative. I'm *not* book smart, but I am good at other things. I just hope that my new tutor can help me get my grades up, or I'll be royally screwed."

"Shit, I didn't realize you were struggling that bad," Brando murmurs.

Chase waves him off. "It's fine. This year has just been harder than normal. The last two years were fine. I kept the grades I needed to, but this year, the information isn't sticking like it has in the past."

"Is your tutor helping so far?" Brando asks.

Chase's cheeks turn a bright shade of pink, and he tilts his head from side to side. "Kind of, but he's also really fucking cute, and it's kind of distracting."

Brando and I chuckle. "If he's too distracting, find someone else. Don't let your dreams suffer because of a cute face," Brando advises.

Chase laughs while shaking his head. "I won't let that happen. Besides, he's *not* into me, which I really don't get..." He pauses and moves his hands up and down his body. "I mean, look at me, what isn't there to like?"

"I hate to break it to you, kiddo, but there are more important things in life than good looks," Brando explains to his cousin, who doesn't look convinced.

"That can't be true," Chase counters. "Anyway, I'm sure I'll figure it out. This guy is hella smart, and I think he's the only one who will get the information to stick."

"I've got faith in you," Brando replies. "And if you need anything, let me know."

"Will do," Chase assures him. "Now, where is all the signed stuff you promised me?"

Brando leads his cousin over to the rest of the guys, who are holding the signed items, and Chase shakes each of their hands before pausing for a photograph.

"Thanks for all of this," Chase says, preparing to leave while the band gears up for the official meet and greet.

"Ready to meet fifty of your fans?" I ask Archer as Chase walks away.

"More than ready. I love these events," he tells me with a killer grin, and I'm almost desperate to kiss him, but I can't yet. So instead, I put my hand on the small of his back, guiding him down the hall.

The event space is already set up when we arrive, and the band sits at a table while we let in the fans. Once things are steady, I stand beside Archer at the end of the table. Right now, a blonde with sky-high heels is standing in front of him, gushing about how much Country Skies' music has meant to her.

"Oh, before I forget, some dude stopped me outside and wanted me to give this to you," she says, reaching into her bag to pull out a present.

"This isn't from you?" I question, stopping Archer from accepting the gift.

"Nope, but I mean, not everyone has the budget to afford meet-and-greet tickets, so I thought it would be nice of me to bring it in for him," she explains with a genuine smile.

"That was very sweet of you, but I'll have to take that from you and open it at a different time," I tell her, taking the wrapped box. "Do you happen to remember what the guy looked like?"

She shakes her head and shrugs. "Sorry, it was kind of dark outside. He noticed my special badge and told me how jealous he was," she says, holding her lanyard. "He seemed like a nice guy."

"I'm sure he was," I assure her, even though it's a lie. "But it's protocol for our security team to check unknown gifts."

"Makes sense."

The rest of the guys finish signing her poster, and she leaves with a giant grin on her face.

"Do you think that's from my stalker?" Archer asks in a hushed tone.

"I'm not sure, but we'll open it later," I tell him, and it's obvious he's nervous now.

I don't blame Archer for feeling off, but I am thankful the stalker didn't somehow get into the meet and greet. Not knowing who this person is, is driving me nuts. We have a description of the guy who drugged Archer, but we don't even know if that's the same person who is sending the creepy letters and gifts, and that makes things difficult.

The rest of the meet and greet goes off without a hitch, and by the time we get back to the bus, everyone is tired and ready for some sleep. We'll be driving through the night to get to the next venue, but tonight isn't over yet.

Brando, Landon, and Joseph head to their bunks, and Aria, Archer, Rip, and I get comfortable in the main living area.

"What do you think it is?" Aria asks, pointing to the gift I've placed on the table.

"I don't have a clue, but we're going to find out."

Rip puts on a pair of cut and needle resistant gloves, just in case, and begins opening the present while the rest of us wait with bated breath.

After the wrapping paper is off and the box is open, Rip pulls out what looks like an old-school microphone, but it has arms and legs and is holding a guitar. It's a simple decorative item and not creepy, but it has Archer gasping.

"What?" I ask him, studying his face carefully.

"Didn't Mom buy that for you when you got your first gig?" Aria asks, and Archer nods, his hands covering his mouth and his eyes wide with fear.

"It disappeared a few months ago. I didn't think anything about it, thought maybe the cleaner moved it, and kept forgetting to ask about it." He takes a deep but shaky breath. "The guy was in my house."

"Is there anything else?" I ask Rip.

"You're not going to like this," he grumbles, pulling out a pile of photos and handing them to me.

There are about fifteen different pictures of Archer and me together over the last couple of weeks, and it has my blood running cold. The images aren't anything to out our relationship, but this fucker has been following us, and I've been none the wiser. How is that even possible?

Thankfully, none of the pictures are from Archer's house, which means the security system hasn't been breached, but it has me second-guessing myself. I'm normally well aware when people are watching me.

"There's also this," Rip states, handing me a piece of paper.

My dearest Archer,

You've always meant the world to me, but it seems like I don't mean the same to you. How is it possible that you are giving your heart to someone else? Have my gifts meant nothing to you? Good thing I'm patient and willing to wait out this little fling. I hope you don't mind that I borrowed this. I wanted to make you another one that is more special, and I needed the original to know how to make it perfect. I look forward to giving it to you in person one day soon.

Until then, sending all my love,

~X

"This is getting out of hand," Archer grumbles.

"He won't get anywhere near you," I assure him.

"But he was already in my house," he argues.

"*Before* we installed your security system and before I was assigned as your bodyguard," I remind him.

"But he's now been stalking both of us and somehow knows about our relationship, all while neither of us knew he was even there. How is this happening to us?" His voice breaks, and tears well in his eyes, so I pull him into my arms to comfort him.

"We're going to find him, and I will never let him hurt you," I promise, praying it doesn't turn into a lie.

When things start to escalate with stalkers, they can get sloppy but even more dangerous. My entire team needs to be on high alert now. I refuse to let a hair on Archer's head be touched by this psycho.

"I'm ready to go to bed now," Archer states in a quiet and defeated tone that has my heart breaking for him.

"That's enough for tonight anyway. Rip, can you give Nixon the CliffsNotes' version of what's happening and tell him I'll give a full report in the morning?"

"On it," he confirms. "You two get some rest."

I grab Archer's hand and pull him to our room at the back of the bus. It was nice of the band to allow us to share the large bedroom. I guess in the past, they've used a bus with an office instead of a bedroom in the back since no one had a partner, but this time, they went with a more traditional style so Archer and I could sleep together.

"Can you hold me close tonight?" Archer requests after I've shut the door.

"Always," I promise. "Are you okay?"

He shrugs and lets out a deep sigh. "I'm not sure. If I'm being honest, I am scared. I was kidding myself into not believing things were this serious. But now I can't pretend it was just some isolated incident and not a real danger. I get it now and understand why you all have been so worried."

Archer's body almost curls in on itself while he talks. His arms are wrapped around his middle, fingers clenched tight, and fisting around his T-shirt as he looks at the floor.

Pausing to take a deep breath, he raises his eyes to mine before continuing. "I'm really glad you're here with me, but I'm also upset that you're being targeted now too."

Tears stream down his face, and I pull him into my arms, kissing his cheek and squeezing him tighter to me. I pull back and cup his head in my large hands. Using my thumbs to swipe away the wetness that kills me to see, I meet his glistening eyes again.

"None of this is your fault," I remind him with a firm tone, leaving no room for arguments. "Whoever this asshole is, they are unhinged. No matter if we were in a relationship or not, I bet this person would feel threatened that I'm around you so much. He might not even know I'm your boyfriend. We've done a very good job of keeping our distance in public. He's only saying what he's thinking. He doesn't have any proof."

"It still sucks," he complains quietly into my neck. "And here I was thinking about asking you to make our relationship public, but that probably isn't a good idea now, is it?"

"It actually might be the best idea," I counter. "Yes, it will piss off your stalker, but it has the possibility of getting him to act, and that would mean getting him arrested sooner rather than later."

"Isn't that dangerous, though?" he questions, leaning back slightly but still holding onto me tightly.

"Yes," I reply, refusing to lie to him. "But we'd have a plan in place, and we have an amazing team with us. I'll talk to Nixon about it in the morning. In the meantime, let's get some rest."

We both step away from each other to undress and shut off he lights. The second we are under the covers, Archer is in my arms, clinging to me like I'm his lifeline. It breaks my heart that he's going through this. Dealing with stressful and dangerous situations is my job, so I'm used to it, but Archer isn't and shouldn't have to be. No one deserves to have someone invade their privacy like this.

I run my hand up and down my man's spine, praying we'll be able to devise a plan to catch this guy so he stops playing mind games with Archer.

I refuse to let my man get hurt, and I will do *anything* to ensure his safety.

Chapter Twenty

ARCHER

THE BLARING OF AN alarm wakes me from my restless sleep, and I pull the blankets over my head, praying for another hour of rest. To say I slept like shit last night would be an understatement.

Obviously, I was completely aware I had a stalker and there was a possibility they would try to get at me during the tour, but I attempted to push it to the side of my mind, not letting it get to me. Unfortunately, the gift last night makes it all too real. Before, it was just an idea, and I had foolishly convinced myself that the stalker would move on. But now it's clear they haven't, and I'm more than a little freaking out.

"Do we have to get up now?" I grumble as Bennett tries to slip out of bed.

"You can stay and rest, but I need call Nixon. I forgot to put my alarm on vibrate so it wouldn't wake you," he tells me, and I pout, which Bennett kisses. It almost makes everything better. Almost. "I'll be back soon. You try and go back to sleep."

I snuggle into the blankets as Bennett gets dressed, then slips out the door, leaving me alone. The room is still dark and quiet except for the gentle sound of the bus traveling down the highway. You'd think it would be perfect for sleeping, and it typically is, but I can't seem to close my eyes.

Being by myself right now feels wrong, so I slink out of bed, pull on a pair of sweats and a comfy sweater, and make my way toward the main living area.

"Would you like some coffee?" Aria asks with bags under her eyes. I guess she didn't sleep well, either.

Nodding, I plop myself beside Bennett, leaning my head against his shoulder.

"Would you like me to put the call on speaker?" he checks with me.

I lift a shoulder. "Might be easier," I reply, then a giant yawn slips past my lips, and I slap my hand over my mouth. "I'm gonna need a nap at some point today."

Bennett kisses my forehead before calling Nixon on speaker. As we wait, I cuddle into his side, needing to be close to him right now.

"Good morning," Nixon answers after a couple of rings.

"Morning," Bennett replies. "I've got you on speaker. Archer and Aria are with me."

"Rip still sleeping?" Nixon asks.

"Yup, I figured I should let him get all the sleep he can get as things seem to be going crazy around here," Bennett notes.

"Yeah, it sounds like it. You make sure you get lots of rest too," Nixon tells him.

"I'll do my best," Bennett mumbles, but I'm not sure I believe he's going to take a break on his own, so I make a mental note to drag him to bed with me after this call is done. I'm not sure I'll be able to actually sleep without him, so it's for both our benefits.

"Is there anything we can do for you here?" Nixon asks after a brief silence.

"I'm not too sure yet, but I've been toying with the idea of pissing the stalker off deliberately," Bennett states.

My brows pull together, still hating the idea, but Nixon chuckles as if the idea doesn't sound insane, or maybe Bennett is known for crazy plans.

"And how exactly were you planning to do that?" Nixon questions, and there isn't any anger in his tone. It's more amusement, the exact opposite of how I feel.

"Right now, all the stalker is showing are images of Archer and me in public. We don't know that he's actually aware of our relationship. There's the possibility he's only assuming right now. If we officially announce our relationship to the public, it could make him go off the deep end. There's also a strong chance he'll try something radical, but we would be ready and waiting," Bennett explains.

The line goes quiet briefly, giving us all a little time to think about what Bennett just said. My skin crawls at the idea of Bennett being more of a target because of me, but by how confident he sounds, I don't think there will be any way to deter him.

"Are you ready to make your relationship public?" Nixon eventually asks.

"I was thinking about it all day yesterday *before* the gift. I'm pretty sure I am, if Archer is," Bennett says, causing my heart to race.

"I was thinking about it too. I'm ready if you are," I assure him, and a giant smile spreads across my handsome man's face, filling my chest with warmth, almost alleviating my anxiety around the idea of goading the stalker. "But only if it's safe. I refuse to put either of us in extra danger if there is another way to do things."

"Honestly, I don't see the risk being that much greater," Nixon states. "You have a fantastic team with you, and the stalker is already talking about seeing you in person again soon. If the announcement does trigger him, he won't be as calculated in his actions, and it will give our team an advantage."

"I can get our PR team on a call in the next half an hour if this is what we want to do," Aria suggests.

"I'm on board with this plan if both of you are as well," Nixon tells us.

"I'm in," Bennett replies, looking into my eyes with an intensity that almost makes me dizzy.

I close my eyes and take a deep breath, putting my faith in my man and his team. If everyone is positive this is a good idea, who am I to say no? My eyelids flutter, and I smile at the man who already means the world to me. "Let's do this."

Bennett leans in to kiss me, and I melt into him. I wish we were alone so I could deepen the kiss, but we aren't, and there is too much to do right now. Maybe later we'll get some alone time. At least we'll be staying in a hotel tonight.

"Would you like to be included in the call with the PR team?" Bennett checks with Nixon after breaking the kiss.

"I have another meeting this morning, but please fill me in on the plan once it's decided. I trust your judgment, especially in a situation like this," Nixon states.

After we say our goodbyes, Aria is immediately on her phone planning our next meeting.

"Are you sure you're ready for this?" I ask Bennett quietly, more nerves curling deep in my gut. "You know it's going to be chaos once the public finds out about us."

Bennett beams at me as he looks deeply into my eyes with an expression that instantly puts me at ease. *How is it possible that just one look can ease almost all my worries?*

"I'm well aware that it's going to be chaotic, but I'm prepared," he assures me. "Not being able to touch you in fear of someone seeing is driving me crazy. Yes, I had originally wanted to keep things on the down-low for longer, but I'm over that now. And if us letting the public in on our relationship doubles as a step in catching your stalker, then that's just a bonus."

The corners of my lips turn up, but right as I'm about to kiss my handsome man, Aria clears her throat.

"Enough with the fuck-me eyes," she scolds, and Bennett chuckles. "Hillary is getting everyone together. We'll have a conference call in about fifteen minutes to come up with the best plan of action. I'm going to brush my teeth and put on another pot of coffee. Do you want to have the call out here or in your room for more privacy?"

"Here is fine. We don't need privacy from the guys. They know what's going on and will support us in whatever we decide to do," I tell her.

She yawns as she stands, and I pray we catch this stalker as soon as possible because seeing my sister tired and worried like this is killing me.

Chapter Twenty-One

BENNETT

IT'S KIND OF SURREAL listening to Archer's PR team rattle off ideas and tell us what to do. I'm normally the person coming up with the plan of action, so to be on the receiving end is a bit of a mind fuck. But they are the experts, and Archer trusts them, so I'm inclined to do the same.

"The first thing we should do is post a teaser picture to your social media pages," Hillary suggests.

Aria nods. "Maybe a selfie of Bennett kissing Archer's forehead, but most of his face cropped out to be mysterious," she adds.

"I love that," Hillary exclaims gleefully.

"I'm on board with that," I reply.

"Maybe the caption could read *Traveling is the hardest part of touring, but some things make the time pass quicker*," Archer states.

Aria's eyes light up with delight, and her head bobbles up and down. "That's perfect."

"After that post, everyone will be dying to figure out who your new man is, and it won't take them long to start digging around," Hillary says through the phone sitting on the coffee table. "If you *really* want to give them something to talk about, you could go out to a restaurant or bar after the show, and we can tip off the paparazzi. All Bennett would have to do is place his hand on Archer's back, and the internet will blow up with gossip. Then you can wait a few days while the rumor mill works and make another social media post with Bennett's full face."

"Sounds like a solid plan to me," I note, and Rip dips his chin in agreement.

"Could you give me a heads-up of the restaurant? I want to make sure we get the layout and communicate with management that we'll be there," Rip requests, and I can't help but smile for thinking exactly as I would if I were running lead.

"I'll get that to you shortly," Aria tells him. "Are you okay with the plan?" she checks with Archer.

"Yup, seems easy enough," he replies.

With everything settled, I text Nixon fill him in on the plan, and Archer leans into me. "Ready for a selfie?" he asks with a waggle of his brows.

I chuckle. "Get your phone out."

After he does, I press my lips to his forehead as he angles his cell to cut most of my face out of the picture.

"What do you think?" he questions, both of us staring at the image.

"It's perfect," I assure him.

Archer beams at me, then creates a post in an app that allows him to post on all his social media accounts at once.

"I've got you reservations at a high-end steak house tonight after the show," Aria tells us after the post goes live. "I've also sent the information on the restaurant to both of you," she informs Rip and me.

I smirk. "Thanks for realizing I'd want the details too."

She giggles. "I might not have known you long, but even someone without eyes can see that you're a control freak. Obviously, you trust your team, but there is no way you are going to take Archer out tonight without being involved in every step of the safety measures."

I shrug. No sense denying the truth.

"Is this your first time having security yourself?" Archer asks.

"I'm not having security tonight," I argue.

"You kind of are." Rip steps in, and I narrow my eyes. "What?" He lifts his hands in defense. "You won't be the head of security tonight when you go out for dinner. The team is going to be there to protect Archer *and* you, whether you like it or not. The stalker is *not* a fan of yours, which means in a situation like this, you are the client too."

I huff out a breath and cross my arms, possibly acting like a petulant child but not really caring.

"It's okay to let people take care of you," Archer whispers.

"You're one to talk," I counter, making Archer laugh.

"Okay, you're not wrong. I hate the idea of needing protection, but I get it now. I don't know what I'd do if you got hurt because of some crazed fan."

"It's my job, babe," I remind him. "I'd take a bullet for you." I stare intensely into his eyes, trying to show him how serious I am. "But if things go according to plan, I won't have to. While I think the idea of me needing protection is absurd, I'm also not going to push my team away. That's why they are here... to help. And when we are out for dinner tonight, I'll try to put away my bodyguard hat and be present on our date."

Archer's face lights up at my promise, and it makes my heart beat a little faster. This man is so much more than a client. He's my boyfriend, and he deserves my full attention tonight. Thankfully, my team is amazing, and I fully trust them.

"Are you ready to start planning for tonight?" I ask Rip, who smirks at me.

I may trust them, but I will make sure we are as prepared as possible.

ARCHER STRUTS ACROSS THE stage, singing to his fans and reaching his hand out to high-five people. He looks so in his element right now, and I wonder if his face hurts from smiling so much.

"Check-in time," I say into my radio as the song ends and Archer talks to the crowd.

"All clear near the dressing rooms," Henley replies.

Michael, Carter, and Cole echo the same response for their areas.

"Everything looks good over here," Rip states last from the other side of the stage.

"Michael, would you please come to the stage?" I request. "Archer has been doing more crowd work tonight, and I want one of our guys in that area now." The stadium-hired security is set up there currently and seems to be doing an excellent job, but they aren't a part of my team. Therefore, I can't trust them as much. "Carter, you can cover Michael's hall and yours now."

"On my way," Michael responds, and Carter lets me know he heard the new order.

With the new plan in place, I bump my elbow into Aria's arm. "He's killing it tonight," I tell her, and her smile grows wider.

"I know," she replies. "They're always on their A-game, but tonight it's like something is different. Maybe it's you." She winks at me, and I chuckle.

"I was here for last night's show," I remind her.

She shrugs. "Maybe he's extra excited for the date. Or he's happy that the response to his social media post is so positive."

Saying the post is performing well is almost an understatement. It's blown up in the few hours it's been live, and *everyone* is talking about it. The response has been overwhelmingly positive, so there is a chance that's why Archer is extra energetic tonight.

Almost every gossip website already has posts about who Archer's new lover could be and saying how they are so happy for him. I'll be shocked if they don't connect the dots that I'm the boyfriend before dinner tonight. Hillary and her team are watching the websites like hawks, ready to give us any new information we might need.

"What do you think the fans are going to name your relationship?" Aria asks randomly, and I lift a brow, completely confused at her out-of-nowhere question.

"What are you talking about?"

She rolls her eyes as if I'm an idiot, and who knows, maybe I am. What's safe to say for sure is I'm not as caught up on internet trends as the average person.

"Quite often, when celebrities get into relationships, their fans will create a cute name for them, just like they create names for themselves. Country Skies fans are called Sky Watchers."

Knowing that information already, I nod, but why does our relationship need a name?

"I think they might call you Arnett or Bencher," she continues, and I shake my head.

"Both of those are stupid," I grumble, realizing where she's going with this. It reminds me of Brangelina, which was also a stupid couple's name, but all of them are if I'm being honest. However, people are going to do what they want to do, and it isn't hurting anyone, so I'll go with whatever they come up with.

Archer says goodbye to the crowd a few songs later, and the band walks off stage. The second my man is within arm's reach, he launches himself at me, and I laugh as I catch him, holding him tight.

"You're killing it tonight," I tell him, setting him on his feet again and kissing his lips.

"I know," he responds with wide, vibrant eyes and pure, unfiltered joy written all over his face. "The crowd tonight is feeding my soul like never before."

The fans are still cheering loudly, and Archer and his bandmates quickly down a water bottle each before heading out for their encore. My sexy man gives me a quick peck, then rushes away, and it gives me a lightheaded feeling. I'm so happy we aren't keeping this relationship a secret anymore because I'm already addicted to side-stage kisses and being able to touch my man whenever I want.

Hopefully, my mind won't change after I'm fully thrust into the limelight later tonight.

Chapter Twenty-Two

ARCHER

My heart is racing as Rip drives us to the restaurant in the rental SUV he picked up when we got into town. I'm so eager for this dinner but also nervous as hell.

The internet sleuths have already figured out that Bennett is my boyfriend and are more than a little excited about it. There is a massive debate currently over what our couple's name is going to be, and it makes me giggle every time I show Bennett the suggestions because he thinks it's the dumbest thing ever. I, however, find it endearing.

As we pull up to the restaurant, paparazzi are waiting for us, and I take a deep breath.

"We don't have to do this," Bennett says, looking at me with pinched brows, concern evident on his handsome face.

"I want to do this, but I'm worried this is going to scare you off," I mumble.

Bennett places his hand under my chin and tips my face to his. "Nothing. Could. *Ever*. Scare. Me. Off," he assures me, punctuating each word so I know how serious he is.

My breath catches in my lungs at his words. This is a huge statement for him to make, considering he wasn't even sure he was ready for a relationship only a few weeks ago.

"I'm sure this is going to take some getting used to as I've never been the one people are taking pictures of, but it will be worth it in the end because I get to be with you. If I didn't want to be in the limelight ever, I wouldn't have allowed what we are building to start."

His words put me at ease. "Okay, let's do this."

"We're ready," Bennett says into the radio he's still wearing. There was no point in arguing for him to remove it because it gives him more of a sense of peace, and he needs that right now.

Henley opens the door to the SUV for us, and I gasp at what feels like hundreds of cameras flashing at me. People are yelling, but with so many talking at the same time, I can't actually make out anything being said. Michael clears a path for us, and Bennett escorts me into the restaurant with a hand on my back, which helps calm me.

"There are more paparazzi here than I thought there would be," I whisper as we follow a waiter to our table in a corner near the back of the restaurant, away from prying eyes.

"I'm not surprised," Bennett notes as we take our seats. "Hillary told us she was going to leak the location, and with how crazy people seem to be about our relationship, I honestly thought there would be more."

When he puts it like that, it totally makes sense. I guess I'm just not used to it. Obviously, I'm used to the lack of privacy, but I'm also not the most sought-after celebrity, and I'm thankful for that. Right now, our relationship will be a hot commodity, but hopefully, that will die down soon. I don't want to get used to that many people always following me.

"How are you doing with all of this?" I ask Bennett after a beat.

"So far, it's fine. I'm used to protecting celebrities with big followings, so the paparazzi doesn't bother me, but it's a little strange already reading the stories about us. I didn't realize how fast things would snowball."

I sip my water and then say, "I didn't either. I'm not often the center of gossip magazines, so this is going to take getting used to even for me. I haven't experienced anything like this since my coming out," I admit. "Thankfully, the response this time is more positive overall."

Bennett reaches across the table and places his hand on mine, bringing a smile to my lips. "I'm sorry that anyone reacted poorly when you came out. You didn't deserve that. But I'm also glad people are in your corner this time."

"So, which couple's name do you think is going to win?" I question, changing the subject. He groans, and we both laugh. When he doesn't respond, knowing I was trying to lighten the mood, I note, "This place is really nice."

"I've definitely never had a first date at a place like this before," Bennett replies. "Well, a first public date."

"So far, this is the best date of my life. Period," I tell him.

He quirks a brow at me in response. "Have your previous dates been that bad?"

"Not really. They were okay, I guess. But nobody has made me feel like you do," I admit.

Bennett's smile is soft, and his eyes are filled with adoration that has me melting. "I feel the same way," he replies. "I'm so lucky to have found you."

My heart beats faster at his words, and emotion fills my chest. I'm so fucking lucky to have found Bennett. Not only do I trust that he's going to keep me safe against the stalker, but I'm also pretty positive my heart is safe with him too. This is a good thing because, at this moment, I'm certain it already belongs to this handsome man.

"If you could be any animal, what would it be?" Bennett blurts out, making me snort as I laugh.

"I think an Australian Cattle Dog because they have lots of energy like me, but what's with the random question?"

"It's our first date, so we're supposed to get to know each other better," he explains with an easy grin, and I fall a little more for him.

"Okay, so what animal would you be?"

"Totally a pigeon," he replies deadpan. "I would shit on anyone who's pissed me off."

His answer pulls a full-on belly laugh out of me, and a few people turn to look at us, but I don't care. I tune everyone else out, keeping my sole focus on the sexy man in front of me, who has me smiling so big my face hurts a little.

Humor has always been something I found important in a partner. I don't want to live my days with someone who can't make me laugh.

Every moment I spend with Bennett shows me that he's exactly the type of guy I've been looking for. I only wish it hadn't taken a crazed stalker to bring the two of us together.

We continue asking each other ridiculous questions and spend the rest of the evening laughing together as we get to know each other on a different level. Every new thing I learn about Bennett makes me fall for him a little more.

I've been nervous about giving my heart away after my ex smashed it, but I trust Bennett not to break it. He knows what it's like to have a broken heart, and he never would have agreed to a relationship if he planned on hurting me. He's different than anyone I've ever been with, and I can't wait to see how things progress with us.

I was hoping that by the time we finished our meal and paid our bill, the paparazzi would have moved on, but of course, that would be like wishing for a unicorn. It's not going to happen.

When we walk out, Bennett has his arm around my waist, keeping me as close as possible as his coworkers clear a path for us. Even though

I hate the invasion of privacy, nothing could wipe my smile off my face. I'm so happy to be with Bennett, and there isn't anything that could bring me down from cloud nine.

"Tonight has been perfect," I tell my man once we are in the privacy of the SUV.

Bennett's face lights up, and he leans in for a kiss. It's passionate but simple since Rip is driving and there isn't a privacy screen. As much as I want to jump into my boyfriend's lap, I also don't want to give his coworker a show.

"The restaurant was fantastic, but the night isn't over yet," Bennett tells me, his voice lower and more gravelly than normal. His eyes are filled with want, and it has my body heating, ready to be alone and naked.

"Oh?" I question, playing coy. "What more is there to do?"

When Bennett growls and leans in to nip at my ear, my cock is instantly hard as steel, and a shiver of anticipation runs down my spine as he licks my neck. His tongue is wet and warm, but my skin is cold and exhilarating when he blows on the trail.

"When we get to our room, I'm going to fuck you so hard you'll be feeling me for days," he whispers into my ear.

My dick throbs in my pants and leaks like a fucking sieve. Breathing becomes a little harder, and my heart races as I envision us together.

Would it be wrong to ask Rip to speed?

Chapter Twenty-Three

BENNETT

THE INSTANT THE HOTEL door shuts, I grab Archer, pull him to me, then spin us around, slamming him up against it and smashing my lips to his. He gasps at my sudden movements, and I use the opportunity to thrust my tongue into his mouth, lapping at his and grinding our pelvises together.

I swallow his mewls from the exquisite friction our bodies are making but become frustrated by all the clothing barring his skin from mine.

"Need you... naked... now," I say between our kisses, unwilling to let my lips leave his completely while wrestling with the button of his pants.

Archer pushes away from me. I detest the idea of any distance between us, but it's necessary for getting us naked faster. Keeping our eyes connected, the same heat and need reflects in his that I am sure are in mine. As soon as our clothes hit the floor, I pull him into my arms again and return to devouring his mouth.

I automatically put one hand to the nape of his neck and thread it into his hair, grabbing a tight hold, while I use my other hand to pull him into me by his waist before sliding down to grab a handful of his tight ass. Using my tight hold on him, I grind our cocks against each other, making us both groan. Archer's body willingly submits to the movements of mine, and I relish in his eagerness to give me what I want right now.

I don't always want to dominate in bed, but clearly, I need to right now. Giving up control at dinner tonight had been hard for me, but it was worth it. The price for it seems to be my overwhelming need to demand and control our pleasure now.

The growing slickness between us coats our cocks, thighs, and stomachs as we both leak profusely. Reaching between our bodies, I grab hold of both of us and firmly fist our dicks together.

I groan as Archer eagerly thrusts into my hand, sliding his length against mine. I've always loved a good frotting session, but with how my balls are already tingling, I know I won't last long if we continue like this.

"Bed," I command, letting go of our erections and hissing from the sudden lack of pressure.

Archer doesn't waste a second and rushes toward the bedroom of our suite. When I enter, my cock bobs at the sight of my sexy man lying down and staring at me with a lust-drunk look.

"Come closer to the edge," I demand, moving toward him and kneeling in front of the bed.

He moves at a rapid pace, and once he's in position, I push his legs up, giving me better access to his perfect pucker. I lick my lips before diving in for a taste of delicious cake.

"Fuuuck," Archer cries out as I eat his ass.

I circle my tongue around his hole a few times, then stiffen it and shove it inside him. His cries of pleasure fill the room, and knowing how thin hotel walls are, there is a strong possibility whoever is in the next room can hear him. The idea of someone listening to us fucking turns me on even more and makes me want to see how loud I can make Archer get.

I lift my right hand and swipe my index and middle fingers over Archer's rock-hard cock, collecting his precum to use as lube so I can stretch him. *Fuck, I love how much he leaks for me.*

With my fingers coated, I bring them to his entrance and slide one in along with my tongue.

"Jesus," Archer breathes out, his back bowing while I fuck him with my mouth and finger.

"You're so fucking delicious," I tell him, then slide in my second finger and lick his perfect dick from root to tip, swirling my tongue around the sensitive crown when I get to the top.

The saltiness of his precum explodes in my mouth, and I moan around him, swallowing him down my throat.

"Holy shit," Archer shouts, and I smile as much as I can with my mouth so full. "Fuck. Fuck. *Fuck.*"

He continues to shout, moan, and cry out while I bring him as close to the edge as possible.

Damn, I fucking love how loud of a lover he is.

"P-please," he begs.

I pop off him and tug his balls to stop him from coming yet. "Are you desperate for your release, baby?" I ask, and he nods, panting profusely.

I chuckle at how overcome with desire he is and walk to my suitcase to grab the bottle of lube I packed. His precum might have been enough to lube my fingers, but I don't think it would be enough for my cock, and I don't want to risk hurting him.

With the bottle in hand, I strut back over to my man, who's watching me with hooded eyes. "Are you ready for me to fuck you like I promised?" I check, pouring lube onto my cock and stroking my length a few times, making sure I'm nice and slick.

"Please," he pleads again. "Fill me up and fuck me hard. I need you to take me."

My cock bobs at his words, and a low growl rumbles up my chest. "With fucking pleasure," I tell him, lining myself up with his entrance.

Archer wraps his legs around my waist when I push inside him, and we both groan as his body sucks me in. My eyes roll into the back of my head, and as I slide into him again, I praise him. "Oh fuck, you're perfect."

The instant I'm balls deep inside the man who has stolen my heart, the edge of my desperate need for control melts away. This feels so damn right. I release a contented sigh and lean down to kiss him, giving him a moment to adjust to my size.

Our tongues dance with each other, and his channel pulses around me. It has me needing to thrust before too long.

"Fuck me," Archer begs when we break for air, and I do exactly as he asks.

After I push up so I'm standing and grip his hips firmly, I dig my fingers into his flesh and pull my hips back, then slam them forward again. Archer's cries become higher pitched as I fuck him hard and fast. Sweat drips down my spine, and my heart races while I chase the high we both desire.

"You were fucking made for me," I grit out, thrusting in and out of him as hard as I can. "You're mine, and no one else will ever get to be with you for as long as I live."

This possessive desire to mark him takes over me, so I lean down again, this time to bite his pec hard but not letting up on my pace. The move has Archer crying out and his cock leaking even more.

My spine tingles with the need to release, so I grip Archer and jerk him off, my hand matching the pace of my hips. It doesn't take long before my man is shouting, and his cum is coating our bodies. As his release takes him over, his channel clamps down around me, and I instantly blow, filling him with my load and almost collapsing from the intensity of the orgasm.

After a few heavy, gasping breaths and we have both regained our equilibrium, I kiss him gently, then slide out, watching my cum seep from his hole. It's so hot, and I'm glad we decided to go without condoms.

I'll never get sick of this sight.

On shaky legs, I rush to the bathroom and wet a cloth, then return to my sexy man, who is half asleep already. I give him a quick wipedown, grab his hand, and pull him up with me.

"I think we should have a quick shower before we sleep," I tell him as he rests most of his body weight against me.

"Fine," he grumbles. "But make it quick, or else I'm probably going to fall asleep in there."

I chuckle, guiding him to the bathroom. "I promise I'll make it quick. All you have to do is stand there and let me clean you."

He mumbles his acceptance while I turn on the shower and wait for it to warm up.

"You're too good for me," he says softly once we are under the spray and I'm holding him close.

I shake my head and kiss his cheek. "Absolutely not."

There are three precious words on the tip of my tongue, but it seems too soon to say them. We haven't even been dating for a month, but I know it's how I feel.

As fast as possible, I wash both of us, making sure to pay extra attention to Archer's sensitive hole. True to his word, he leans his body into mine, his breathing evening out. As soon as we're clean, I wrap us up in towels and drag my tired man to bed.

Knowing I fucked him so good that he's basically asleep on his feet does something to me.

The moment his body touches the bed, he melts into it, and once I'm beside him, I pull him into my arms. Archer rests his head on my chest, and I lazily trail my fingers up and down his spine.

It's so evident to me that this man is it for me. I know I'm going to love him for as long as I live, and I'll be by his side for as long as he'll have me.

As Archer's breath evens out, and I'm certain he's asleep, I whisper, "I love you."

Maybe in the morning, I'll find the courage to say the words when he's awake.

Chapter Twenty-Four

ARCHER

THE MORNING LIGHT SEEPS in through the sheer blinds, waking me earlier than I would have liked. We don't have to be anywhere until this afternoon, and I wanted to sleep in, but we forgot to close the blackout curtains last night.

Bennett stirs next to me, wrapping his arms tighter around me. "Why didn't we close the blinds?" he grumbles.

I titter. "We were a little preoccupied when we arrived."

He hums out a response of agreement and pushes his hips forward, which has his morning wood pressing into my ass.

"Care for another round?" The low growl rumbling in his chest makes my cock harden, so I roll in his arms to kiss him, using my lips to tell him yes.

Our bodies rub against each other, and I'm ready for more in no time, but before we have a chance to take it to the next level, Bennett's phone rings.

I groan. "Don't answer it," I urge him, but he's already reaching for the annoying device to check who's calling.

"This better be an emergency," Bennett answers and clicks to place the call on speaker.

"You know I wouldn't call unless it was important," Rip tells him.

"What is it?" Bennett asks, sitting up.

I sigh. *Guess the time for shenanigans is over.*

"Another gift showed up this morning," Rip explains.

My blood runs cold at his words. *Why the fuck does this keep happening?*

"So, he is following the tour schedule," Bennett muses out loud.

"Seems like it, but we already figured as much," Rip replies.

"Who has that kind of money?" I question. It can't be cheap to travel around the world with a band.

"He could be bumming rides," Rip suggests.

"We're gonna get dressed," Bennett says, rubbing his forehead. "Meet us here in ten."

After he disconnects the call, he sends texts to Aria and Nixon to fill them in on what's going on. Aria, of course, responds that she's getting dressed and not to start without her.

"What do you think the gift is this time?" I ask, climbing out of bed and heading to my suitcase to pull on a pair of sweats and a hoodie.

"Hard to say, but I doubt it's going to be anything good."

I nod, pulling the soft material over my head. As soon as I'm clothed, I pad to the living room area of the suite and drop onto the sofa.

"Whatever it is…" Bennett continues once he's joined me on the couch, "… it's going to be fine. We won't let this lunatic get close to you. I promise."

The corners of my lips turn up a hair, and I lean into the man who has vowed to keep me safe. His strong arms instinctively wrap around me, and I let out a contented sigh. I might be on edge right now, but this embrace is keeping me grounded.

Bennett holds me until Aria and Rip show up, and my stomach rolls at the sight of the perfectly wrapped present.

"The note is on the outside this time," Aria states.

"I noticed that as well, which makes me even more leery of the gift," Rip replies, and my body shakes with dread.

Donning his cut and needle resistant gloves, Rip opens the letter and reads it out loud.

"My dearest Archer... I already knew of your betrayal of our love, but I merely thought it was a fling and nothing to be concerned about. Yet here you are now, flaunting this affair in my face. How do you think that makes me feel? I have done nothing but love you, and yet here you are, stabbing me in the heart. While I'm utterly heartbroken right now, the love that I feel for you remains, and I'm willing to forgive you. We can still be together like destiny has planned. I won't give up on you, and I promise I'll do whatever I need to be with you."

"Well, that's not creepy at all," Aria mumbles sarcastically.

"I don't think I want to see the gift," I whisper as a ball of emotion lodges in my throat.

"We can open it somewhere else," Rip offers.

Bennett looks intently into my eyes, asking me silently if that's what I want.

I'm having a hard time answering because I'm afraid. What if the gift is more of a threat against Bennett? I was on board with the plan to announce our relationship, knowing it would piss off the stalker, but I didn't realize how much of a target that puts on Bennett.

Now I'm second-guessing everything. I won't be able to live with myself if something happens to Bennett because of me. But refusing to look at the gift won't change anything, and if my boyfriend isn't backing down, I can't either.

"No, open it here," I say after a moment.

Rip stares at Bennett, waiting for the go-ahead. Once he gives the okay, Rip carefully unwraps the box and pulls out a miniature house.

"That's not as creepy as I thought it would be," Aria voices exactly what I was thinking.

"It's a replica of my house," Bennett states, the color draining from his face.

My eyes go wide, and it's suddenly hard to catch a breath.

"There's something inside it," Rip points out and lifts the roof off to check out what it is, but as soon as he does, the house catches fire, and my scream fills the room.

Rip drops the replica to the floor and quickly stomps on it, putting out the fire as fast as possible.

Bennett holds me close since my body is shaking uncontrollably, and Rip calls the front desk to let them know what happened.

"I need to call Nixon," my man tells me, reluctantly letting me go.

I nod, unable to speak at the moment. Bennett stands, heading to the bedroom, and Aria takes his place on the couch, wrapping her arms around me.

"I'm sorry this is happening," she whispers.

"Me too," I respond, my voice breaking.

"Does the front desk know who brought the gift in?" Aria asks Rip as she rubs her hands up and down my back in a soothing manner.

"I asked this morning, and they said it was a Maria Hadley," he tells us. "They had to get someone in to access the security footage. The person apparently arrived a couple of minutes ago, so as soon as Bennett gives me the green light, I'll head down to check it out. I'm assuming this is another situation of someone thinking they were being kind, not knowing the real truth."

When Bennett comes back into the room, his hands are shaking, and he looks extremely pissed off.

"What's wrong?" I ask, immediately standing and racing toward him.

"While I was on the phone with Nixon, we both got a notification that there is a fire at my house," he tells me before pulling me into his arms.

I cling to my man and try to wrap my brain around what's happening. "How?" I ask. "Isn't the stalker here? He can't be in two places at once."

"He's clearly got accomplices," Rip grumbles.

"The security footage shows a person in all black starting the fire and running off," Bennett tells us. "The fire department has been dispatched and are on their way. Nixon is going to meet them there and report back on the damages."

"Are the cameras still live?" Aria asks.

Bennet gives a slight nod of his head. "Yeah, but I don't want to watch my house burn. Fuck, now I know how Knox felt, but at least I wasn't *in* the house when the fire started."

"I'm so sorry," I cry out into his chest. "This was a stupid plan."

"It's going to be okay," Bennett tries to reassure me. "No one was there, and it was just a house. You're safe, I'm safe, and that's all that matters."

"But what if it doesn't stay like that? What if you get hurt?" I ask as the sudden urge to punch a wall courses through my veins. I've never felt such a strong rush of fear and anger in my life, and I don't know what to do with it. I feel like this is all my fault, yet as hard as I try, I can't think of a solution to the problem.

"We have an amazing team with us. We will do everything in our power to make sure no one gets hurt," he tells me, but I don't miss the fact that he isn't promising anything.

"I'm going to run down and check out the hotel's security footage, and hopefully, we can contact the woman who dropped off the package," Rip explains.

Bennett nods at his coworker. "Go. I think Archer and I need a moment alone."

"I'll get out of your hair too," Aria says, walking out with Rip.

"How does someone get so obsessed like this?" I question as Bennett moves us back to the couch, keeping me in his embrace the entire time.

"I'm not sure, but I promise I won't let this asshat touch a hair on your head," he vows.

"Don't think I'm not picking up on the fact that you aren't promising that *you'll* be safe too."

"My job is to protect *you*."

His words set me off, and I pull out of his grasp to poke him hard in the chest. "You're not *just* my bodyguard, or have you forgotten?" I yell. "You're my boyfriend, and if you want to make sure that I'm not hurt, you'll keep yourself safe too. Because even though we've only been together for a short time, I'm already certain I'm in love with you, and it would *destroy* me if you were taken from me now."

Shit, that's not exactly how I was planning on telling him I love him, but it's out there now, and I refuse to take back the words. I meant them, even if I said them while shouting.

"I'm sorry," Bennett whispers, shaking his head. "I guess I wasn't thinking about how my getting hurt would make you feel. I had tunnel vision about keeping you safe no matter what. I love you too, and I promise I'll try my hardest to keep us both safe, but I'm also not going to lie to you. If it comes down to me or you, I'd sacrifice myself in a second."

There isn't anything more either of us have to say, so I move in for a kiss, needing his touch more than anything and showing him how much he means to me with my body. I think we both need this right now—the connection and security of being together.

"As much as I'm dying to fuck you silly right now, I need to brief my team on what's going on," Bennett tells me when we break for air. "We'll need tighter security tonight, and as much as it pains me to say this, I shouldn't be the lead right now. Rip will have to take the reins until I'm less of a threat. But don't think that means I'm still not going to be by your side."

I'm disappointed that we aren't going to do the horizontal tango, but I understand Bennett's need to talk with his team, so I offer him a small smile. "I wouldn't expect anything less. I need to hit the gym. Do you think you can have your team meeting there?"

"I'll call the front desk to make sure we can lock down the gym for an hour," he states and moves to pick up the receiver.

After the front desk gives the okay, Bennett texts his team, and I go into the bedroom to change into my workout gear.

"Everyone will meet us in the gym in fifteen minutes," Bennett informs me as I'm pulling on my shorts.

"Sounds good to me. Could we still head there now so I can start warming up?"

"Yup," Bennett says and holds his hand out for me.

"You're kind of the perfect boyfriend," I tease, taking his hand in mine.

He pulls me into him and plants a sweet kiss on my lips.

I could get used to this man in my life forever.

Chapter Twenty-Five

BENNETT

ARCHER RUNS ON THE treadmill as my team and I sit on benches, reviewing tonight's new plan. Rip is taking the lead, as I already informed Archer, and I'm having a harder time than I figured I would be letting him do so.

The man I love's life is in danger, and I can't be in charge of keeping him safe because I'm also at risk. It all fucking sucks.

"We need to be on high alert tonight," Rip reminds everyone. "The meet and greet has been canceled, and the band members are to go directly to the airport after the show."

Originally, the plan was for Archer and his band members to drive to the next location, but we don't know how much the stalker knows, so we need to change up the plans as much as possible.

"I've already sent an email to the stadium's head of security, requesting more personnel to do rotating shifts of the areas the band members normally are in while they are performing so our team can be closer to the stage," Rip continues. "We are to take all threats seriously, and if for any reason we think the risk is too high, the show will be called off."

Archer doesn't want to cancel the show, but I'm with Rip on this. My boyfriend's safety is our number one priority right now, and we won't be taking that lightly.

As Rip continues to walk the team through their new roles, I try to pay attention, but my focus keeps veering to Archer, who is now lifting weights.

How is it that in less than three weeks, this man has become my world? I wasn't expecting this, but I'm happy it happened.

My phone buzzes as the conversation wraps up, and I swiftly answer the call from Nixon.

"What's the update?" I ask.

"It's not as bad as we expected," he replies, and I let out a sigh of relief. "It's still going to need major repairs but seeing as it's a newer house without any debris outside, the fire took longer to get rolling. Thanks to your security system, the fire department was alerted immediately and showed up in time to put it out quickly."

After one of my colleague's houses caught fire about a year ago, Nixon implemented new rules for the rest of us. One was that all Hunter Security staff members were to have alarm systems with at least two cameras. The second was that all homes must be fire-smarted.

It's two easy steps that seem to have worked well.

We were praying something like this wouldn't happen again, but clearly, it never hurts to be prepared.

"Repairs are a hell of a lot easier than replacing a whole house."

Nixon hums his agreement. "The fire chief is going to email you the report when it's done so you can forward it to your insurance company."

"Any clues as to who the person is?"

"I wish," he replies, sounding frustrated. "The person's face was mostly covered, and their clothing was baggy. It's impossible to tell if it was a man or a woman. The police are canvasing the area, but I doubt they are going to find the person."

Great, another dead end.

"I'm surprised that this person is coming up with plans like this and has people helping them," I murmur.

"Same here. But this person is clearly not well. Maybe they've convinced their friends or family that whatever they are thinking is the truth."

I grab the back of my neck, wishing we knew more. "If you get any more information, let me know," I say after a brief pause.

"You know I will," Nixon assures me. "Keep your guard up, and remember you are a target now too. Let Rip take the lead, and if he tells you to do something, listen." His tone has no room for argument, and even though I hate it, he's right.

"I will," I grumble.

I place my phone back in my pocket and look at Archer, who seems to be finished with his workout. "All done?" I check, standing and making my way toward him.

His face is red from working hard. "Yup, now I'm ready for a shower. Care to join me?" he asks, waggling his brows at me.

Even though I'm feeling extremely stressed out, I can't help but laugh. That's something I've noticed about Archer. His presence alone sends this rushing force of peace through me. I've never felt anything like it before him. It's how I know he's meant for me.

"I'd love to join you," I reply, pulling him into me for a passionate kiss.

"And that's our cue to leave," Henley says, and the rest of the guys respond with their agreement.

"Don't forget there are cameras in here. Might want to save the hanky panky for your room," Cole teases.

"Hanky panky? How old are you?" I question, and Archer chuckles.

"Twenty-two, but I'm an old soul," he replies with a hand on his chest as if touching said soul.

"I'm pretty sure hanky panky is a term reserved for boomers," Rip tells him, but Cole doesn't let that sink his spirits. He does, however, stick his tongue out, proving that he is indeed a child.

"On that note, we'll be leaving," I tell them, taking hold of Archer's hand and leading him into the hall and toward the elevator.

Rip tags along to escort us to our room. A part of me is dying to argue about him shadowing us, but deep down, I know it's a necessary precaution. It doesn't mean I have to like it, no matter how much I trust Rip and my team.

"Nixon informed me that my house isn't that bad. It will need some major repairs, but the fire department got there fast, and the fire didn't have that much time to grow," I tell them, getting them up to speed as we get into the elevator.

"That's great," Rip replies.

"Repairs are easier than having to build an entire new house," Archer adds, clearly on the same wavelength of thinking as I am. He tries to smile at me, but it doesn't reach his eyes. It's obvious he's still blaming himself for the incident.

It doesn't matter how many times I try to assure him it isn't his fault, he's still going to harbor some guilt about the situation. So, instead of wasting words, I'm going to use my body to make him forget—at least as soon as we're alone. I might have unlocked a new kink of people hearing us while we fuck, but I don't think I'm quite an exhibitionist just yet, especially not in front of my friend.

"Text me when you're ready," Rip states after we arrive at the room and he's done a quick sweep of the space.

Now that we are aware the stalker knows which hotel we are staying at, it's important to check each time we leave and come back. It's a pain in the ass but necessary.

"Will do," I confirm, waving at my friend as he leaves.

"Shower time?" Archer asks when we are finally alone.

Instead of using my words to answer him, I smash my lips to his, walking backward and guiding him to the bathroom with our mouths locked together.

My sexy country star is quick to strip out of his sweaty clothes while I turn on the shower and follow suit as the water warms.

"You're so fucking hot," Archer muses out loud, licking his lips.

I smirk, placing my hands on his hips. "I'm nothing compared to you," I counter, kissing him again to cut off any response he might have had. Without breaking the kiss, I move us into the shower, thankful there isn't a tub to stumble over.

"Fuck, that feels amazing," Archer groans as the hot stream washes over us.

"I can make you feel even better," I assure him, dropping to my knees and taking his growing erection into my mouth.

As his hands find purchase in my hair, a deep moan escapes his lips. I smile around his length, loving how it's growing in my mouth.

I work my way up and down him, sucking gently and swirling my tongue around the crown when I get to the top. His sighs and groans of pleasure echo against the shower walls, my cock leaking between my legs.

After fumbling for the bottle of lube we stashed in here earlier, refusing to let go of my man's perfect cock, I pour a little onto my fingers and play with his pucker.

"Jesus," he cries out as I shove my index finger into his tight channel while swallowing him down my throat at the same time.

There is something so heady about making a man like Archer come undone.

As Archer gets louder and his knees start to shake, I use my free hand to stroke myself, wanting to come at the same time as him.

"I'm close," he informs me.

I pop off him for a second, sliding my finger out of him, and he gasps with wide eyes.

"I'm not stopping, sexy," I assure him. "But I want you to let go. Fuck my face and give me every last drop of that load you've got trapped in those balls."

His mouth hangs open as he pants for air, but then he nods rapidly, and I take him back into my mouth. It doesn't take him long to do as I instructed, and his hands grip my head tighter as he bucks into my mouth.

As he fucks my face like a wild man, I stroke my cock, trying to match the rhythm of his thrusts. With each thrust that hits the back of my throat, I swallow, using the muscles to constrict around his thick cock.

"You're t-too fucking good at this," he stammers as he jack-hammers into me.

My head spins at the approach of my orgasm and the lack of oxygen, but before it becomes too much, Archer shouts and explodes in my mouth. At the taste of his salty cum, my release takes over me, and I cover the shower floor with my load.

I make sure not to let a drop from him go to waste and only release him when he's an oversensitive, whimpering mess.

"You sure know how to bring a man to his knees," Archer says.

I rise, pulling him into my arms, and smirk. "I thought I was the one on my knees there," I tease, and he smiles before bringing me in for a kiss.

I'm sure he can taste his release on my tongue, which I find so fucking hot. If I were a younger man, I might get hard again from that thought, but this forty-one-year-old's cock is spent and won't be ready to go for at least a little while.

"Let's get washed up and lie down for a nap," I suggest.

"That sounds amazing," he responds dreamily.

We make quick work of cleaning ourselves, and the moment we're in bed and I have Archer in my arms, I wonder if it's too early to move in together. Because I don't want to ever spend another night without this man in my arms.

Chapter Twenty-Six

ARCHER

EVERYONE IS ON HIGH alert as we walk from our dressing rooms to the stage. I'm praying our performance won't be hindered by our nerves.

After our nap, we told the guys about what was going on, and to say they were pissed would be an understatement. However, what shocked me the most was Landon's suggestion that we cancel the show. He's performed with a broken leg and twenty-four hours after having his appendix removed—he isn't the type to want to cancel. It took some convincing, not only him but the rest of the guys, which I wasn't prepared for. Thankfully, they agreed with me, and here we are about to perform for the sold-out crowd.

Bennett is holding my hand tightly, scanning the area as we go. I try to offer him a reassuring smile, but it's obvious he's stressed.

"No crowd work tonight," Bennett reminds me as we wait backstage for our openers to finish their set.

I give him a quick peck on the lips. "I promise to *just* sing tonight."

I'm sure someone will write a nasty review about me being cold or something, but they would understand if they knew what was happening.

Our openers exit the stage, and we high-five them as they pass, congratulating them on a job well done. As the crew gets to work switching stage equipment, I bounce around, trying to get the blood flowing while going through a few vocal warm-ups.

"Ready to kill it?" Aria asks when it's our time to go on.

"You know it," I respond with a wink, then give Bennett one more kiss before following the guys onto the stage.

The crowd roars as we wave and find our spots, the positive energy almost enough to have me forgetting everything that has been happening. As we start the first song, I get into the zone and push away all the worries and stress I've been harboring all day. I let the music wash me clean and pour my soul into our amazing fans.

As promised, I don't high-five anyone or bring anyone on stage, but I do try to interact with the audience as best I can by reading their signs out loud and taking more breaks to talk and tell stories.

We're about halfway through the set when Aria's voice comes through our in-ear monitors. "Wrap up the song and get off stage."

My sister's voice is cold, and it sends shivers down my spine. I try my hardest not to show how worried I am, but I'm not sure if I'm successful. With a nod to Joseph, we finish the song without repeating the chorus like we usually do.

Then, flashing a false, carefree smile to the audience, I grab the mic while the guys exit the stage. "It looks like we are having some technical difficulties, but we will be back right away," I tell the crowd, then rush to join everyone backstage.

Immediately, I know it isn't good. "What's going on?"

"There is a car parked outside the exit we were planning on leaving through tonight, and a member of the venue's security team found a small explosive in a garbage can down one of the backstage halls," Rip informs us.

My steps falter, and Bennett places his hand on my back so I can continue walking. I'm sure all the color has drained from my face, along with my body heat. I've never felt this cold in my life. Fear is taking over, and I'm not sure what to do about it.

"Marcell, the venue's head of security, is about to make an announcement informing the audience to evacuate, but we wanted to get a head start first," Rip adds, and I nod, unsure what to say.

"This is fucked," Brando murmurs as we are rushed down a hall.

I'm about to state my agreement when the loud bang of an explosion deafens me.

"Shit," Bennett yells, wrapping his arm around me tightly.

"The east exit was just taken out," Rip informs us a second later, and we all run. "Check the exit for explosives!" He's shouting into his headset to Henley, who is already at the exit waiting for us.

Another explosion goes off. This one we can visibly see, but thankfully, it's far enough away it doesn't hurt us.

"Jesus fucking Christ," Rip yells, and we change paths to take another exit since the one we planned to take is now not an option.

"Henley, report," Bennett says into his headset as we race to find a way out.

My heart is racing so hard that I'm becoming lightheaded, but I can't give in. I have to fight through it.

Rip and Bennett look at each other for a moment, sharing a silent conversation that makes my stomach roll. I don't think Henley reported, and I'm not sure what that means.

"This way," Michael shouts, and we follow him through a door.

"This is just a storage room," Rip growls out, but Michael shakes his head.

"I thought the same thing, and it used to be, but it's a hall to a loading dock now," Michael informs us. "It's not on the blueprints we were given because it's too new. I found it when I was doing hall monitoring at last night's performance."

No further arguing is required, and we follow Michael out of the secret loading dock exit. Then Rip instructs the driver to our new location.

As we make our way outside, another explosion goes off. At this point, I don't know where it is.

"That car just went up in flames," Bennett tells us.

All of a sudden, a rush of people is racing by us, pushing and shoving as they go, separating some of us. Bennett's hand stays strong in mine, and I know someone would have to cut his hand off before he ever let go.

"Where the fuck is the car?" he yells.

There are too many people for me to tell where any of our friends are, and when I realize I don't know where my sister is, my chest aches as panic takes over my body.

"We've got to follow the crowd," Bennett instructs me when, out of nowhere, a gunshot echoes throughout the night, making my ears ring.

People panic even more now, pushing and shoving like crazy, but that's when I realize Bennett isn't moving us along, and instead, I'm being dragged down.

"Bennett," I shout, crouching beside my man as he clutches at his neck.

Blood pours from the wound, and I push my hand against it, trying to think of a way to stop the bleeding. As I keep pressure on the wound, I feel a hand on my arm, pulling me up again.

"Don't think about fighting, or I'll kill you too," a man tells me, pressing something hard against my back.

When I look up, I'm face to face with the man who drugged me, and I don't know what to do.

"I don't want to kill you, but I fucking will. Now move," my stalker yells.

Tears burn at my eyes as he drags me along. The only chance I have at saving myself and Bennett is to go with the flow for now, so I stop fighting and go through the crowd with a deranged man, all the while praying that someone stops to help the love of my life.

Panic threatens to take over, but I keep my eyes peeled, hoping to find a way out of this situation.

As we mingle with the crowd, I finally spot a familiar man to my left. If I'm right, it's Marcell, so I try to make eye contact with him while not alerting the stalker to my plan.

Look at me, I scream inside my head. *Fucking* look *at me*.

We continue walking, and I'm afraid Marcell isn't going to catch on when, finally, he turns his head and our eyes lock.

Help, I mouth, pleading with my eyes for him to have a plan. His brows shoot up, and he gives me a nod before saying something into his walkie-talkie.

Our pace never stops, and I eventually lose sight of Marcell. I can only pray that whatever plan he has works.

When I look forward, I see the crowd starting to thin out ahead, meaning we are getting far enough away from the danger that people can disperse. Unfortunately, it also means this man is likely to take me to another location, even farther away from any chance of being saved.

I am trying not to panic, but my heart is racing, and I feel it throbbing in my throat. I look around wildly, searching for any way to get free. Willing myself to take deep breaths, I try to dispel some of the adrenaline fog in my head so I can think more clearly.

Suddenly, the people behind us become aware of the thinning crowd ahead and become impatient, pushing and shoving their way forward. The force of so many people hits against me hard, but it manages to knock me out of the grasp of the stalker. Without even thinking, I turn to flee. It's now or never.

Knowing I can't go with the crowd since it's the way we were headed, and trying to go back would be pushing against the tide of people, I push sideways, opting to let them move around me.

I don't get far when I hear the man shout "No" at the top of his lungs, and two gunshots go off.

Pain pierces through my shoulder, and I drop to the ground, clutching the bullet wound.

I'm expecting the stalker to catch up to me, but he doesn't show. Instead, it's Marcell who crashes to his knees beside me.

"We've got to get you to an ambulance," he states, taking his shirt off and pressing it hard against my shoulder.

I nod, and he helps me stand. When I turn my gaze back toward where my stalker was, Marcell urges me to walk.

"You don't have to worry about him anymore," he assures me.

I'm not sure what he means. Is the guy dead, wounded, or maybe in custody? I'm not sure what outcome I am hoping for more. A part of me wants him dead so that no matter what, I'll never have to see his face again, yet another part thinks that's the easy way out and he doesn't deserve that.

"Do you know how Bennett is?" I ask Marcell as we walk toward some flashing lights.

He shakes his head. "I know he was taken to a hospital, but I don't know more than that."

That isn't much to go on, but at least if he was taken to a hospital, there is hope he's still alive.

"What about the rest of the security team? Were any of them hurt in the explosions? What about my band and my sister?"

"Everyone is accounted for," Rip states, walking up to us. His words settle my nerves a little, but I still have more questions. "Get in the ambulance, and I'll fill you in on everything else."

The paramedics get me situated as I wait for Rip, who is talking with Marcell, before climbing in with me.

"How is Bennett?" I ask when I have Rip's attention, and I'm no longer being poked and prodded.

"He's in surgery. So is Henley. That's all I know."

I gasp. "When he didn't report in over the radio, I thought... I don't know what I thought, but Henley's alive?"

Rip nods. "Yes, and hopefully, when we arrive, there will be new information for us."

"What about everyone else? Where is Aria, Brando, Joseph, and Landon?" I ask, my words tumbling out as my heart races.

"You need to calm down," one of the paramedics instructs.

"Everyone is at the hospital with Carter and Cole guarding them. Michael is following behind the ambulance," Rip tells me, and I try to take a few slow, deep breaths. "Everything is going to be fine."

He sounds like he means the words, but there is no way he can make that promise. Shit happens so fast, and things can change at the flip of a dime. I won't believe everything will be okay until Bennett is next to me, holding my hand and smiling at me.

Rip focuses on his phone for the rest of the ride, and I keep wondering what will happen when I get to the hospital. Obviously, I'll get checked over and stitched up. I'll be fine in the long run, but what about Bennett and Henley?

If we arrive and I'm told they didn't make it out of surgery, I don't think I'll be able to handle it. If *anyone* other than the stalker dies tonight, I'll never outlive the guilt.

I should have canceled the concert as everyone urged me to. I would have, had I known things were going to get this bad. But I was a fool and once again only thought about myself. I figured the threat was still *only* against Bennett and me. I never fathomed that the stalker would go to such extremes and risk hurting so many other people.

The ambulance ride is quick, and when we arrive at the hospital, I'm swiftly given an X-ray, where it is confirmed the bullet went directly through my shoulder, missing the bone and anything major. Then I am escorted into a private room to get stitches and antibiotics.

"THANK FUCK YOU'RE ALIVE," Aria cries out when she barges through the door as the doctor is leaving. I'm surprised it took her this long to gain access to the room.

Tears are streaming down her face, and I know without a doubt I've never seen her this hysterical before.

"How are you?" I ask, trying to get the focus off me.

"Not fucking well," she replies honestly. "I've been trying to distract myself from worrying by working with Hillary on trying to gain control of the narrative. Social media and the news are obviously all over this story."

"Oh shit... were any fans hurt?" I question, and my stomach rolls, hoping like hell she'll say no.

"No major injuries and no deaths," she assures me. "There are a few people who got banged up since panic set in after the first explosion, but thankfully, the venue security was on it and took control of the situation fast. They ensured no one was trampled and that everyone got out as safely as possible."

I blow out a sigh of relief.

"Any news on Bennett yet?" I check, even though the doctor already promised he would send someone in as soon as they knew more.

Aria shakes her head, staring at the floor. "How did this turn into such a shit show?"

I wish I had an answer for her, but I don't, and who knows when we'll get them?

She sits on the side of my bed and holds the hand of my good arm. "We'll get through this together like we always have," she whispers, and I nod.

Aria will always hold me when I crumble, but is that going to be enough to get me through the pain if I lose Bennett?

Chapter Twenty-Seven

BENNETT

Beep. Beep. Beep.

Someone needs to shut that fucking beeping off.

Beep. Beep. Beep.

Where the hell is it even coming from?

The annoying noise doesn't stop, and I'm ready to throw whatever it is out a fucking window. But when I try to move, it's like my body weighs three thousand pounds. It's not like one gains that much weight overnight, so something is obviously off. Even my eyelids feel like they are tied down by weights.

I keep trying to force my eyes open as the beeping continues, but more noise filters through. People are talking around me, but I'm having a hard time making sense of the words. It all sounds like gibberish, and that can't be right.

Finally, after what feels like an hour of trying, my eyes open, and I'm greeted with bright fluorescent lights, causing me to squeeze them shut again.

Where the fuck am I?

My body shivers, suddenly freezing, and my face is damp from tears streaming down my cheeks, even though I'm not sad.

"It's okay," the soothing voice of my man tells me. A voice I could never forget.

Archer's hand slides into mine, and I focus on how calming his touch is.

After a couple of deep breaths, I open my eyes again, this time focusing on the sexy country star at my side. As his face comes into focus, memories come rushing forward, and I squeeze his hand tighter.

"S-s-s." I'm trying to say stalker, but my throat is on fire, and I'm struggling to get the word out.

"Shh, rest your voice," Archer tells me. "Your doctor is on his way. He'll explain everything."

I nod but regret that decision as a throbbing pain erupts.

How the fuck did I survive being shot in the neck?

"Mr. Carter, it's good to see you awake," a man with a stethoscope around his neck says as he enters the room. This must be my doctor.

"Can he have water?" Archer asks. "He tried talking, but I think his throat is raw."

"Of course," the doctor replies, turning to a young woman in bright pink scrubs. "Can you get a glass of water for Mr. Carter, please?"

She nods with a smile, then leaves the room.

"Do you know why you are here?" the doctor asks me.

"Mm-hmm," I murmur, not wanting to try full words yet but also wanting to keep my neck still.

"That's good," he says reassuringly. "When you were shot, the bullet went through the side of your neck. It severed your carotid artery, which normally would have had you bleeding out."

I'm sure my eyes are comically wide right now. *How the hell did I get lucky enough to not die?*

"Thankfully for you, someone in the crowd knew to pinch the artery shut," he continues. "I've never seen roach clips used for something like that in all my years of being a doctor, but it worked. I'd like to know how this passerby knew what to do, but it's my understanding that he disappeared when the paramedics showed up.

"When you arrived at the hospital, you were rushed into surgery for an arterial graft. The surgery went well, and we were able to remove the damaged piece of your artery and replace it with a flexible hose that will act as a blood vessel.

"We're going to keep you here for at least another day or two to make sure you don't show any signs of infection. You're going to have a pretty significant scar, which is nothing compared to the alternative. But... as far as we can tell right now, you're on the road to a full recovery."

I'm stunned as I take in his words. I am one lucky son of a bitch to be alive right now.

When the nurse arrives, Archer takes the cup from her and brings the straw to my lips. I take slow sips, relishing in the relief the cold liquid offers.

"Thank you," I whisper to the doctor who helped save my life.

"Of course. On a scale of one to ten, what is your pain like right now?" he asks.

"Seven," I answer honestly. "And I'm really cold."

"That could be from the anesthetic wearing off," he explains. "The nurse can top up your meds to bring the pain down and get it under control. I'll make sure someone brings in another blanket. Right now, the most important thing you can do is rest."

"I'll try," I respond and try to smirk at the doctor, which thankfully brings a smile to Archer's handsome face.

"I'll make sure he does," Archer assures the doctor.

"I'll check on you in the morning," the doctor states, then leaves.

The nurse gets to work putting more medicine into my IV line while another comes in momentarily to drop off another blanket as promised. Archer and the nurse spread it over me, and I instantly feel warmer.

Before leaving, the nurse meets my eyes and gives me a stern look. "It's important that the meds stay ahead of the pain. At the first sign of discomfort, tell me. There is no place for tough-guy grin-and-bear-it nonsense here. You get me?"

I want to chuckle because she obviously has me pegged, but I give her a small smile and attempt to tip my chin in agreement. She nods, lets me know to press the button if I need anything, then leaves to check on other patients.

Archer helps me sip more water, but then my eyelids become heavy again as the meds kick in, and it becomes ridiculously hard to keep them open.

"Rest," Archer tells me when he notices my struggle. "I'll be here when you wake. I'm not going anywhere."

As promised, when I wake, Archer is by my side, and even though I'm sure sleeping in a hospital chair wasn't comfortable, I'm happy he stayed.

"How did you sleep?" he asks.

There are bags under his eyes, and a small yawn slips past his lips, so it's evident he didn't sleep well.

"Not bad, but I missed having you cuddled against me," I tell him, and he grins.

"I promise once you get out of here, you won't be able to get me out of your bed," he replies, leaning down for a gentle peck.

"I hear someone's awake," Rip says, tapping on the door frame of the hospital room.

When he enters, I notice he's not alone. The guy with him looks familiar, but I'm struggling to put a name to the face.

"Do you remember Marcell?" Rip asks, and it finally clicks. He's the venue's head of security.

"It took me a second, but I do now," I reply. "Please tell me you have some answers as to what the hell happened last night."

Marcell's face drops. "I do, but first, I want to apologize for failing everyone last night," he starts but pauses to swallow down his emotion. "I pride myself on running a tight ship, and yet someone was able to enter the stadium, plant bombs, and shoot two people." His voice cracks at the end, so he clears his throat before continuing. "The police have identified Archer's stalker as Samuel McGilvery. He gained access to the stadium with the stolen identification tag of a newly hired janitor, George Conroy. Samuel beat George the night before the incident and left him for dead in his apartment."

Archer gasps and covers his mouth.

"George will live, and the stadium is vowing to make sure all of his medical treatments are covered along with paying him during his recovery," Marcell adds. "I was the one who rescued Archer last night, shooting Samuel to get him away. I wish I'd been faster so that Archer wasn't shot too."

I turn to my man and only now realize his left arm is in a sling. Tears prickle behind my eyes. *I failed him. He could have died because I didn't see Samuel soon enough.*

"Don't you dare blame yourself," Archer grits out like he's reading my mind.

"I only intended on wounding Samuel, but my shot was lethal. So, I'm afraid that some questions we have will never be answered."

I nod, letting his words sit with me for a second. I'm not upset that Samuel is dead. People like him can rot in hell for all I care, but I don't love that there are unanswered questions. It's always going to feel like we're missing pieces to this puzzle.

"I do have the answer to one question, though, and hopefully, this information will put your minds at ease," Rip butts in. "Samuel's accomplice was caught and arrested. It was his idiot brother. He was bragging about the fire at your house in a bar. The owner overheard the conversation and called the police.

"The second he was brought in, he confessed to the entire thing and even ratted on Samuel. He claimed to not know *why* Samuel was obsessed with you but said he never second-guessed anything his brother told him to do. Unfortunately, the conversation only happened while the explosions were going off.

"Nixon phoned me as soon as he was notified. I guess he tried to call you as well, but we're not sure if that was before or after you were shot."

"At least we don't have to worry about these incidents continuing," I murmur, feeling a rush of relief at that.

"If you want more closure, you can watch the interview for yourself," Rip suggests, and I nod. That probably isn't a bad idea. "The police will be coming by to interview both of you today. They interviewed everyone else last night, but I was able to ask them to come back for the two of you and Henley, using your injuries as excuses."

I gasp. "Henley's alive?"

Rip's lips turn up. "Yes. He was crushed by a wall that fell during the explosion, which caused massive damage and broken bones. Things were touch and go during his surgery, thanks to his internal bleeding, but they were able to get it under control, and he's now recovering.

He'll have to stay in the hospital longer than you, but they have high hopes that he'll make it through."

"Thank God," I reply, some of the weight lifting from my shoulders and making breathing easier.

"That's how I felt when I heard the news last night," Archer tells me. "The only person who died last night is Samuel, and the world is a better place without him."

I smile at the man who has changed so much in me. "Now we can build our relationship without a looming threat over us."

He chuckles. "Yes, and I can't wait."

Chapter Twenty-Eight

ARCHER

We had to cancel five shows, but we're back on schedule now, and I'm excited to perform, even if I'm missing my man like crazy.

I wave at our fans as I walk across the stage for our first show since the incident. The crowd's roar fills my soul and gives me this intense rush of joy I experience every time I step on stage. It's a high I love chasing. The only other time I feel like this is when I'm in Bennett's arms, where I know I'll be soon enough.

Much to Bennett's dismay, he's at home resting for at least a month, or until I feel comfortable with him coming on the road again. His recovery time is roughly four to six weeks, and if he would rest, it would probably be fine for him to tour with me, but that's not his personality. Since my injuries didn't require surgery, being back on stage a week later isn't a big deal. I only have to dial things back for the time being.

"Let's get this party started," I yell into the mic, and the crowd loses their shit. The noise is so loud it almost outpowers the band, so I tap on my ear, signaling the audio team to turn my in-ear monitor up.

Once I can hear the music properly, I perform like my life depends on it, and it feels so fucking good.

"HOW WAS THE SHOW?" Bennett asks when I answer the video call from my hotel room.

"It was amazing," I tell him. "But I missed you like crazy."

"It's been less than twenty-four hours," he reminds me with a smirk.

"Yes, but it's going to be at least a month before you're on tour with me, and even though I know it's necessary, it will not be easy to be away from you for that time."

"You could change your mind," he suggests.

I laugh and shake my head. "We both know that's a horrible idea. I'm willing to rest and take it easy when I am not on stage. You would refuse to do that if you were here, and you'd end up hurting yourself."

He scoffs. "Fine. Then we'll just have to be creative in our ways to stay close," he says, his tone flirtatious.

"What did you have in mind?" I ask.

"Prop your phone up on your nightstand and get naked," he instructs.

I obey without putting up a fight, but as much as I want to rush and get naked as soon as possible, I'm slow-moving these days.

"I could help get you naked if you let me come with you sooner," Bennett tells me as I carefully remove my shirt.

"Nice try," I tease, dropping my shirt to the floor. Next, I work on my pants. When my belt and button are undone, I push down my jeans and underwear at the same time, kicking out of them once they hit my ankles.

"Fuck, I want to touch that body," Bennett says with a husky tone.

I wink. "Soon. Now it's your turn to get naked."

He smirks at me, setting the phone down and reaching behind his neck to pull his shirt off. My mouth waters at the sight of his warm, rich abs. I want to run my tongue over them.

When he gets rid of his pants and underwear, I'm almost drooling over his perfect cock as it points proudly toward the screen.

Bennett spits in the palm of his hand and strokes himself. "I wish this were your mouth," he tells me as his fist moves up and down his hard length.

I lick my lips. "Soon," I say again, transfixed by his movements.

"Get on the bed and stroke yourself," he orders, but I lunge for my suitcase first, grabbing the bottle of lube.

As soon as I'm in place, I pour some onto my hand before running it up and down my throbbing cock.

"Yeah, baby, just like that," he murmurs, moving to sit on the bed.

The sight of Bennett sitting in my house and on my bed makes me want it to be that way all the time. He isn't officially living with me, but he is staying at my house for the time being while his is being repaired. I don't want him to move out when his house is fixed, though. He belongs with me all the time, and this moment solidifies that for me.

We both watch each other through the small screens as our fists move up and down our cocks, our movements synchronizing as we go.

"I can't wait until we're together again," Bennett murmurs, his eyes never leaving my dick. "Until I'm the one working you like that. Until I can take you into my mouth and suck you dry. Pump into your perfect ass and fill you with my load. You're mine, Archer Dawson."

"Yours," I choke out, picking up my pace, and Bennett follows suit.

"You're so fucking perfect. Everything about you. Inside and out. When we're together again, I'm going to fuck you so hard you'll never forget that you belong to me," he assures me.

I love that he can be sweet *and* dirty at the same time.

"I belong to you, and you belong to me," I add, but making coherent sentences is becoming harder as I get closer to my release.

Bennett nods his agreement. "That's right, babe. I'm yours, and I am desperate to feel you inside me. I want you to straddle my thighs while I lie on my belly. Feel the weight of your cock on my ass cheeks as your hands roam all over my back, shoulders, and neck."

I can see Bennett's cock swell even more as he talks. He looks so sexy right now, with his lust-drunk eyes watching every stroke of my hand on my cock.

I purposely slow my pace, not ready for us to blow so soon.

"Mm... more. Tell me more. I love your filthy mouth. What would I do next?" I ask directly, wanting to hear more of the dirty, sexy ideas that flow through my man's mind.

It's hot as fuck.

Bennett licks his lips before he starts back in again.

"I'm just imagining your hands rubbing all over me as your weight pushes on me and traps my cock against the mattress. It would be an exquisite kind of torture, making my balls ache.

"Then the wet splatter of you drizzling body oil from a height would splash against my body as it falls all over your cock and my ass. But instead of you grabbing your cock and spreading it to coat yourself, you pull my cheeks apart just enough to expose my star."

My cock throbs at his words, and my breathing gets heavier, imagining that what he's saying is actually happening. I'm loving where this story is going.

Bennett has needed to be the one in control in the bedroom recently. I suspect it's because of all the stress we've been under. Now that the threat is gone, it's exciting to see him going to a headspace where he can surrender that control—to me.

We both continue to stroke our cocks as Bennett goes on with his fantasy. "I think you're about to push in, but instead, you wedge the length of your shaft in the trench you've made and squeeze my cheeks around your thick length."

Taking both of his hands, he links his fingers together and surrounds his cock more fully. I copy him, wanting to feel what he feels.

"Fuck, baby, then you start to move... slowly sliding your shaft across my sensitive pucker while the oil spreads."

We both leisurely glide our hands up and down our raging erections.

"Not in a hurry, you shift your body so you can continue to drive me wild with your cock stroking across my hole, but now the rest of you is sprawled over me, holding me down, while your mouth licks... and sucks... and bites at my neck and ears."

I can't help but jump right into this fantasy of his. "Mm, that's right. My cock would be teasing you, making you try to buck your hips into me, wanting more. You'd be desperate to be filled."

Bennett groans in answer.

"That's right, I'd make you moan under me, and when you weren't expecting it, I'd lift my hips higher, notch my head at your eager hole, and push my way in until I'm buried deep inside you, all the way to my balls."

I see Bennett on the screen as his eyes flutter shut and his head tilts back. His words come out in a strangled near whisper. "Yes... oh fuck... yes... Archer, pleeeaaase."

Hearing him so undone has my balls tightening. I'm so close now, and I know exactly what to say that will tip my man over the edge with me.

"Then I'd pull back and slam in and out of your ass... hard and rough. Taking you... and making you... *mine*. I'd pound you so hard that your whole pelvis would slide back and forth on the bed, grinding your cock against it. I'd fuck you like that until you couldn't take it anymore, and you came. You'd come so hard for me that you'd cry out, your body clenching around me.

"Oh... but I wouldn't stop or let up for a second. I'd keep fucking that spasming hole of yours, drawing it out longer and really making you empty your balls. Then, when you were spent completely and collapsed beneath me, I'd up my speed and force just that little bit more. I'd use that sensitive hole of yours to get myself off while you moaned, held down and helpless. Only able to take what I gave you... and I'd give it to you. I'd ride you till I found my own orgasm. I'd bury myself as hard as I could and shoot my cum deep inside you, claiming your mouth with my own."

My words are Bennett's undoing, as I knew they would be.

"Archer... I... I have to... Archer, I have to come... pleeeaaase," he pants out.

The sight of him is my undoing. I call out to him right before my orgasm hits. "Fuck... come for me, baby, squeeze your dick hard... and *come*." I practically shout out the last word as my release jets out of my shaft.

My eyes meet Bennett's as he climaxes seconds after me, his cum covering his stomach in thick sticky ropes like mine did to me seconds before.

"Holy shit," I whisper, giving my heart a moment to stop racing.

"I have to admit phone sex with you is a lot hotter than I thought it would be," Bennett tells me, and I chuckle, wiping myself with the hand towel I stashed beside me earlier. Sitting up, I grab my phone so I can bring it closer.

"Real sex is better, though," I counter.

My sexy bodyguard slash boyfriend laughs. "Obviously, but if this is the only way I can have you for a couple of weeks, then I'm okay with that."

"We both need to rest now," I remind him. "And don't be doing anything stupid while I'm gone, or I'll hire you a babysitter."

His smile has me feeling all warm and fuzzy inside. If I wasn't sure before that he was the one for me, I am now. It's perfectly clear that nothing will keep us from each other.

Not a crazy stalker and not distance.

Chapter Twenty-Nine

BENNETT

ONE MONTH WITHOUT HOLDING the man I love in my arms has been hell, but today, that finally comes to an end.

"Long time no see," Rip greets, wrapping me in a bro hug when I arrive at the stadium.

"It's only been a month," I remind him with a smirk. "But thank you for taking care of my man while I was forced to rest."

"Did you actually rest?" he asks, walking beside me as we make our way down the hall toward the changing rooms.

I titter because he knows me so well. "I did, but only because Nixon was keeping an eye on me and threatened to fire me if I didn't," I grumble.

Rip laughs. "Thankfully, there was no fighting Archer to rest between shows. He's actually good at following orders."

I roll my eyes, but he isn't wrong. "How has the past month been?" I ask, already getting down to business.

"Mostly uneventful," he replies.

"That's perfect," I reply.

He slaps me on the back with a grin. "I figured you would say that. And even though I'm going to miss being in charge, I am happy to hand over the reins."

"How about we say we're sharing the lead on this tour?"

I don't miss the way Rip's face lights up a little at my suggestion, even though he's trying to play it cool.

Arriving at Archer's dressing room, I rap my knuckles on the door frame.

"You're here," Archer shouts, rushing into my arms.

"Fuck, I've missed you," I whisper into his neck, holding him tightly.

"Not as much as I've missed you," he replies, not letting me go.

"Aww, we love a happy reunion," Aria coos from behind us. "Now we won't have Archer whining every day that he misses you. For that, I'm eternally grateful."

"What, you didn't miss me too?" I ask, turning to see her while keeping Archer at my side.

"Maybe a little," she murmurs with a smirk.

"Remember, with Bennett back, you might get more time alone with Rip," Archer tells his twin.

She blushes, and I raise a brow at my man, clearly out of the loop here.

"Mind your own business, brother, or I'll trip you and break your leg," she threatens.

Archer laughs in response, then gives me another hug. "I'll explain everything later," he whispers into my ear.

I kiss his temple, and Aria pipes up to say, "Time to get on stage."

Since I didn't have time to meet with our security team, I'm letting Rip take the lead tonight and am more or less just being Archer's boyfriend tonight. He escorts us down the hall, and we meet up with the rest of the band at the stage.

"Welcome back," Landon greets me. "I'm excited to have you in charge again and not Bossy McGrouchy Pants here."

"I thought you liked it when he took charge?" Aria teases.

Landon blushes, and my brows shoot up once again.

"I'm clearly missing something here," I whisper to Archer.

He smiles. "I just found out last night. I'll explain after the show."

The opening band comes off stage, and the crew gets to work changing out equipment and props.

"Break a leg, handsome," I tell Archer when it's their turn to get on the stage. "But not literally. I need you in the best shape possible for what I have planned for tonight."

He chuckles, giving me a passionate kiss before rushing on to entertain another sold-out stadium.

I'm in awe as he sings to his fans, pouring his heart out. And, like always, watching him on stage spreads a warmth through my core. It's something I will never tire of.

Though I am letting Rip handle things, it's hard for me to stand down completely. Needing to ensure Archer's safety is engraved in me and not something I'll be able to give up entirely.

Everything goes smoothly, and it's like a million pounds have been lifted off my chest. Still, I won't be totally relaxed until I have him alone. So, when he steps off stage, it's no wonder I'm practically pulling him to the waiting car. Thankfully, he doesn't fight me, like he's on the same wavelength as me.

"You killed it out there tonight," I tell my boyfriend on the ride back to the hotel.

I made sure that when I planned my return, it was on a night the band was staying at a hotel. I don't think his band would appreciate us keeping them up all night, and there is no way I will be able to keep my hands off him once we're alone.

"So, what is going on with Aria, Landon, and Rip?" I check with Archer, knowing full well Rip can hear us from the driver's seat.

Rip sighs. "I'm going to have to tan Landon's ass for not being able to keep his mouth shut," he grumbles.

"Do you want to tell me what's going on?" I ask my friend.

"The three of us are sleeping together," he offers.

Archer shakes his head while grinning like a fool. "I think it's more than just sleeping."

"Did you want me to say I was fucking your sister?" Rip counters, and Archer shudders. "It's nothing serious, is all I meant."

"Just don't break her heart," Archer tells Rip in a tone I think is supposed to be menacing but isn't fully coming across that way.

"I'm not planning on it," Rip assures him. "We're all on the same page that this is just fun for the time being. I'm not a relationship guy."

"I've heard that one before," Archer murmurs, looking at me with a knowing smile.

"Sometimes it's worth getting over your insecurities and trying something even if you're scared," I voice.

Rip shakes his head and blows out a breath. "This is why we didn't want people knowing. Just drop it, okay? We're three consenting adults, and we know what we're doing."

Archer shrugs, so I agree to leave it too. It's their lives, and if they want advice, they'll ask for it. That isn't going to stop Archer and me from gossiping about it in private, though. I'm also dying to know *how* Archer found out.

Arriving at Archer's hotel room, I quickly scan the place. Old habits die hard, and once I've confirmed we are safe, I pull him into my arms and smash my lips to his.

"Fuck, I've missed you," I murmur against his lips and lick the seam. I thrust my hips forward, and Archer gasps with pleasure, so I push my tongue into his mouth to dance with his. I break our kiss briefly to nibble on his neck and ear, loving the way my man trembles in my arms.

"Looks like I haven't forgotten how to drive you wild," I note as Archer sighs and moans.

He doesn't respond, which I was expecting, so I continue to lick and nip at his sensitive areas while unbuckling his pants, ready to have him naked *now*.

The moment his cock is free, I drop to my knees, taking him into my mouth and not caring that my dick is trapped in my pants. It's been far too long since I've tasted my man, and I'm starving for him.

"I forgot how talented you were at that," Archer says as he stares at me with hooded, lust-filled eyes.

"Let me remind you of all my talents," I tell him, swallowing him down my throat.

His hands quickly find purchase in my hair, and I hum around him as I come up to the crown and swirl my tongue around it.

"As much as I want to taste your release, I've been desperate for you to fuck me and fill me with it instead," I state, pulling off him with a *pop*.

Archer licks his lips. "Get naked, then get on the bed, sexy," he commands. "On your back. I want to see your face when you come."

I obey him, moving so fast to get naked that I almost trip over my pants. But I don't let the little fumble slow me down. Like I've been given the superpower of speed, I'm naked and on the bed in record time.

Once I'm where he wants me, Archer joins me, also gloriously naked and with a bottle of lube in hand. My cock leaks at the sight of him. His creamy, toned abs and that defined V have me panting. I don't think I have ever wanted a man more in my life.

"Before I stretch you and take you, I need to taste you," he states, lowering himself to his knees.

With firm but gentle hands, he pushes my legs up, giving himself access to my waiting pucker that is dying to have him inside me. His hot, wet tongue laps at me, slowly at first, but it's enough to have my head falling back as a needy mewl escapes from my lips.

"I think I see now why you're so into me being loud," Archer muses, then dives back in for a better taste of my cake.

"Fuck," I cry out when his tongue slides inside me, swirling it into my entrance.

Archer is the king of rimming, and if this were how I was going to die, I would go out a happy man.

After a good amount of licking and nibbling at my hole, Archer pours lube onto his fingers and carefully slides one inside me, ready to get me stretched. While he fucks me with his finger, he sucks my needy, leaking cock into his mouth, and again, I moan with pleasure.

Who knew a month without sex with my man would turn me into this whimpering mess?

Thankfully, Archer isn't much of a sadist, and he works quickly to get me stretched and ready. "Are you ready for me, handsome?" he checks, standing and pouring a generous amount of lube on his ridiculously hard erection.

"So fucking ready."

His smirk is so sexy it has my cock bobbing against my stomach.

"Take a deep breath," he reminds me as he wraps my legs around his waist and pushes against my entrance.

I do as I'm told, and the loudest, neediest moan I've ever uttered rips past my lips as he inches his way inside me. I've missed feeling this full. No number of toys can compete with the feeling of my man inside me.

Archer is slow with his intent, filling me and giving me time to adjust to his size. I'm thankful for that, even though I do enjoy the burn from time to time. After going this long without my man, I need him to take extra care and attention, and Archer is fantastic at that.

I can't wait until I can give this to him too, but it will have to wait until at least the morning. I'm positive my recovery game will not be the best right now.

When Archer is entirely inside me, he leans down for a passionate kiss that has my heart melting for this man.

"I fucking love you," I murmur against his lips.

He smiles. "I love you too. Now, are you ready for me to fuck you silly?" he asks, and I nod.

After righting himself, he presses down on my raised thighs, pushing them to the sides of my body, and begins to piston into me like a madman. And I love it.

"Jesus, you're tight," he notes as he fucks me hard and fast.

"It's been a wh—" I tease, but my words are cut off with a needy moan. "Oh God! Right... there!" I pant out when he nails my prostate. He grins at me as he hits my pleasure spot repeatedly.

My throbbing cock leaks against my stomach, and I'm desperate for a release, but I don't want this feeling to end so quickly, either. Archer notices and grabs my dick, stroking me in rhythm with his thrusts.

"Please, I want to feel you on top of me," I practically beg.

He nods. "Slowly slide back on the bed. I'm not willing to pull out of your body for even a second."

Together, we slide across the bed, giving Archer the room to climb up with me. I spread my legs even wider to accommodate his frame between them.

I've missed this—this connection and his physical comforts. He lays his body over mine so we are chest to chest, and I revel in the feel of him so close. He's in me and on me, surrounding my body and filling me with himself.

Lost in just him and me.

This moment is so damn sweet and loving that it makes my heart squeeze. But it also feels like so much more than that. I swear a part of his soul has entered me and weaved itself together with mine. Just like a part of mine has done with him. It's like I can feel it there, beating and pulsing right along with his heart.

Then his mouth crashes down onto mine in a kiss that is searing in its intensity, so hot it fogs my brain over, and I am lost in it.

Not separating our lips, Archer starts up his rhythm again, rolling his hips so his body stays on mine.

Pulling his face away to look at me, he asks, "You feel that too, don't you?"

I can only nod.

"Thank fuck." A small tear comes to his eye that I gently wipe away with my thumb.

I tug his mouth back down to mine, and we get lost in each other again. The taste of him in my mouth, the friction of his body against my hard cock, the glide of him over my tight ring, and the feeling of fullness each time he is balls deep. It's intoxicating.

I'm hovering right at the edge of my release, and it's like he already knows.

"Come with me," he encourages me.

His words have the power to push me over my tipping point, and I come with a roar.

"Jesus," Archer cries out, joining me in my climax and filling me with his hot load.

Afterward, he collapses the rest of his weight onto me and plants kisses on my neck while we wait for our hearts to slow.

I don't miss that he's kissing my scar. "Thank you for risking your life for me," he whispers, and I hold him tighter.

"I would do it any day of the week. You're the love of my life. You're it for me, and I would do anything for you," I remind him.

He kisses me deeply again, and after a moment, he pulls himself out and rolls off the bed. Standing, he reaches his hand out to me. "Come on, babe, let's get cleaned up, then we can cuddle. I've missed sleeping in your arms."

I chuckle and let him pull me up, a drop of his load leaking down my leg.

We make quick work of showering, and everything feels right when Archer is in my arms again.

"I don't ever want to spend a night away from you again," he tells me as we cuddle in the bed.

"I'm not going anywhere," I assure him.

"Move in with me," he says, bringing a smile to my lips.

"I thought I already was living with you," I tease, knowing that isn't what he meant.

He scoffs. "I mean, after your house is done. Move all your stuff into my place, sell yours or rent it out, doesn't matter... just don't stay anywhere that isn't with me."

I squeeze him a little tighter. "There is nothing I'd love to do more, with the exception of fucking you, of course," I assure him with a cheeky grin. "But as soon as the tour is finished, I'll get the rest of my stuff moved over."

He lets out a contented sigh then kisses my chest.

Archer is my forever, and I'm the lucky man who gets to spend the rest of my life with him.

The End

Thank you so much for reading Bennett! If you loved this story please leave an honest review!

That is all for the Hunter Security World.... for now anyway... But up next is a BRAND NEW SERIES!

If you are a fan of college sports romances this is the series for you!
Schooling the Quarterback (GSU Book #1) *is an m/m college sports romance, featuring a nerdy tutor, and a loveable himbo jock and is coming to Amazon and Kindle Unlimited March 7. Pre-Order Today.*

Also by Laura John

*** Indicates M/M romance

GSU – M/M College Sports Series

Hunter Security Series

Sultry Summer Series

2. Long Summer Nights (A Small town low angst romance)

3. Summer Daze (A Small Town Interracial romance)

4. **Summer Memories (A M/M second chance small town romance)*****

5. **Summer Dreams (A M/M Age Gap romance)*****

Love In Sienna Series

1. Secret Smiles (A friends to lovers rock star romance) *ALSO AVAILABLE IN AUDIO!*

2. Hidden Kisses (An enemies to lovers baseball romance)

3. Guarded Hearts (A New adult, best friends to lovers, single mother romance.

4. Whispered Desires (A single mother, enemies to lovers, age gap, rock star romance)

5. **Confidential Moments (A M/M Baseball romance)*****

6. Clean Slates (A fast burn rock star romance)

7. Tangled Love (A rock star romance love triangle romance)

8. Restless Beat (A rock star romance)

9. Love In Sienna Boxset (Books 1-4)

10. Love in Sienna Boxset (Books 5-8)

Sentinel Protection Duology

1. **Fighting Attraction (A M/M bodyguard romance)*****

2. **Embracing Temptation (A M/M age gap bodyguard romance)*****

Standalones

1. Monster In The Shadows (Dark romance standalone)

2. **Kissing in the snow (A M/M Christmas Novella set in the Sentinel Protection World)*****

3. Afterglow (A kinky brother's best friend romance)

Acknowledgements

THANK YOU SO MUCH for reading Bennett. I really loved writing this book and while it is the shortest in the series it is one of my favorites! I truly hope you love reading it!

Now onto the thank you's. There are always so many people to thank and I really hope I don't miss anyone.

First, I want to thank my amazing team. Without them I would be drowning in a puddle of self-loathing and no book would get finished. Not only so they help keep me organized but they are my sounding board when I think I'm going crazy. They really help me keep my head on straight! Brittany Franks and Suzanne Talkington are the real MVPs!

Secondly, I want to thank my superb Alpha/Beta Readers Mandy, Robin, and Shannon. These ladies are always pointing out the beginning issues and are always available for me to bounce ideas off of. I'd probably still be stuck trying to figure things out if it wasn't for them.

My sensitivity readers for making sure that Bennett and Archer were portrayed properly. J.P Jaxson is an amazing human being that I am so lucky to call a friend and makes sure that I never miss represent the gay community. I love that he calls me out when needed and holds me to a high standard, I wouldn't want anything less. My newest sensitivity reader Crystal was an absolute ball to work with and she taught me a lot of things I didn't know. I will never know what it's like to live as a black person, but I am always trying to educate myself so that I can be a better person. I will never stand for hate or bigotry of any type.

My AMAZING editing team who helped me polish this book and make it as strong as it is today! Chantell, Nay, Nikki, and Kaylene at Swish Designs and Editing were so amazing to work with and I don't think I am ever going to let them go.

My cover designer (who I already mentioned earlier but who also definitely deserves a second mention) Brittany Franks. Brittany is simply the best person in the entire world. Not only is she immensely talented but she's also genuinely the most caring person I have ever met. I truly love this woman with all my heart and am NEVER letting her go.

My family for putting up with me when I put myself on a deadline and go a little crazy.

And last but obviously not least... you... the reader... without you I wouldn't be continuing to put books out! Thank you for your continued support. I love you all so much!

About Author

LAURA IS A STEAMY romance author from Alberta, Canada, who melds love and angst together while normalizing mental illness. She also brings a mixture of m/m and m/f books because love is love. In her books, you will fall in love with her rock stars, bodyguards, baseball players, a small town, a 2SLGBTQIA+ friendly University, and even a hired hit man!

When she's not writing, Laura enjoys reading, going to concerts, hiking, and experimenting with makeup!

You can find Laura online here: